The Tooth Bearer and the Masked Crown

Book II

of

The Tooth Bearer Series

DAVID HOWDEN

DEDICATION

This book is dedicated to my family. My wife Debbie Howden, who told me to write in the first place, and supported my ideas and, as always, to my inspiration in life, my daughter Katelyn. Long may she dream of adventures with Tilly and her friends.

Finally, to you the reader for taking the time to read, and venture forth on the adventure with the Tooth Bearer.

David Howden

The Tooth Bearer and the Masked Crown

CONTENTS

ACKNOWLEDGEMENTS

To celebrate World Book Day 2021, and the anticipated release of this book, we held a competition entitled Gname that Gnome where names were submitted for the character of the Mayor of Crescent City. The winning name of Mayor Maurice, submitted by Natasha Power and her family, was picked from Tilly's hat by Katelyn. A fitting name for the gnome indeed. Thank you to all those that entered.

I would also like to thank Sarah Webb and all those who helped read through the draft editions and especially to my wife Debbie who helped format and market, and put up with the endless read-throughs and talks about my books.

Thank you for all your hard work.

Finally, a big thank you to my daughter for providing her illustrations for this book.

Katelyn, I am so proud of you.

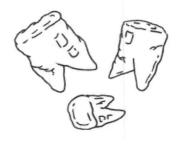

CHAPTER ONE

The whole tooth...

Charlie Goodman was like any eight-year-old that you may pass in the street, well to you and me at least.

To him, beneath the mop of wavy brown hair, round glasses, and freckles, the permanently half untucked school shirt which was held wrinkle-free beneath the handmade knitted tank top; he was a superhero flying through the sky with his cape billowing in the wind or an astronaut on their first spacewalk.

If he wanted to impress his dad for a future career, however..., he'd say he was training to become a lawyer.

That last one was rare, so rare in fact that it was only delivered during family occasions where the remark would guarantee him an extra slice of cake and the chance to excuse himself from the dining room table on Sundays after lunch to do something more exciting.

He believed in many things from Father Christmas to the Easter Bunny, and life was simple. Presents were delivered at Christmas and eggs appeared in his bedroom over Easter, easy.

Now, however, he was being challenged by the eight-year-old girl who sat calmly in front of him, her back straight and with a very serious expression on her face.

"So the teeth are used in the construction industry, for roads and houses and all the bad ones, well they end up in landfill or something like that, I'm not sure really, but you have to look after your teeth Charlie or they can't be used at all and you don't want that, do you?" She spoke quickly and excitedly, the calmness leaving her face as if she had prepared this speech for months, but found that she had only five seconds to deliver it.

Charlie looked at her over his glasses and took a deep breath. He laid the well-sharpened pencil he had been twirling between his fingers onto his desk slowly, whilst the girl delivered her speech.

"Katelyn, the tooth fairy delivers a coin and takes your tooth. That's all there is to it, how do you know the rest?" He spoke slowly and quietly as if explaining a mathematics problem.

The girl in front of him sat back in her chair and sighed. The other children in her class were filing back in from

3

playtime, and that meant school lessons would start soon.

She considered what she was going to say, her voice had already flown out of the window as if it were a bird trapped in a room and had suddenly found freedom. She brushed back her hair from her eyes where it had fallen. In rehearsal earlier, her speech had sounded so much more believable.

Her life had been as simple as Charlie's was a year ago. It was one thing to believe in the tooth fairy, it was another thing to be asked to save them, but that happened when she was seven and an accident transported her to a magical land by a tooth fairy called Tilly Lightfeather.

Her inquisitive nature had kicked in when she touched the magical necklace that the fairies use to teleport between worlds, and the next thing she knew was that she was no longer in her bedroom. Instead, she was in a world populated by fairies, gnomes, sprites, and other creatures she had never seen before.

She discovered she not only had to get home again, a rather difficult feat you might think, but also her baby teeth held the secret to saving the land from something they all referred to as the Darkness of Disbelief, a term she had coined herself when she found out the Darkness was caused by humans forgetting the fairies and their land.

Whilst there, she was told that she was a Tooth Bearer, a person who had special magical baby teeth that, when a full set had been collected, could cast the Darkness that was slowly covering the fairy realm away for a year or two, allowing the fairy folk time to come up with a more permanent plan.

Once the power of the full set of Tooth Bearer teeth had been used the Darkness would slowly return. This meant that another Tooth Bearer would need to be found, and this had been the solution for years.

However, if people believed again as they had many years ago, then the Darkness of Disbelief would disperse on its own. That was Katelyn's difficult mission as a Tooth Bearer, to not only slow the Darkness with her magical teeth but also change the hearts and minds of others. It sounded so easy when she was asked to do it by the fairies.

People had tried in the past to help the fairy realm, and for short periods it had worked. Photographs taken during the early part of the twentieth century had shown fairies playing in gardens and people believed. However, for every photo taken, there was a mob ready to tear the idea down and try to prove that the photograph was fake.

Pictures resigned to the believe-it-or-not section of the newspaper.

"Well, Charlie...," she started, but her words dried up in her throat as if she had been cast into the hottest, driest desert in the world. She coughed and started again. Her hair fell over her eyes again.

"Well Charlie, you see I am a Tooth Bearer and I have magical teeth. When they have come loose and are all collected together and laid out in a circle around this crystal thing, that is in a very tall tower called The Crystal Shard, which is in the City of Landon where a lot of fairies, gnomes, pixies, sprites all live, well...," Katelyn tried to explain.

Charlie looked blankly back at Katelyn through his glasses. She carried on regardless, speaking faster and faster like a runaway train. Even though her voice in her head told her to stop talking.

"The large crystal glows..., I've not seen it happen yet, but when it does it takes the power from my teeth, and 'POOF', the Darkness disappears!"

Katelyn flung her arms over her head as if to show the crystal going 'poof.'

"Only not forever, as it slowly comes back over time and another Tooth Bearer has to be found when my teeth have all been used up. So I am helping by getting people to believe in fairies, which would mean that the Darkness would lift forever and everyone would be happy!"

By now her inner voice was screaming for her to stop talking, leave the room and hide in a corner.

Meanwhile, Charlie's inner voice was telling him to excuse himself politely and go to the toilet, but he was never the person to miss out on a good story, especially when it was someone like Katelyn telling it as she was always so practical and level-headed, until now anyway.

Charlie, against his judgment, had to ask a question.

"So the more people believe in fairies, the more the Darkness lifts forever?"

"Yes, I knew you'd understand, Charlie!" Katelyn jumped for joy in her seat.

"What about the gnomes, pixies, and sprites? Does believing in them as well lift the Darkness?"

"Well, I guess it does...," she said, a little unsure of herself.

"Are you talking to me because I have a wobbly tooth and you think I'm a...?"

"Tooth Bearer, no, the fairies have a special way of knowing when you find one, and you're not one!" she said bluntly.

"Oh…, sorry, that came out wrong. I meant your teeth are very important, but I'm not asking because I think you're a…," her voice trailed off.

"So, you are telling me this story because?"

Before either of them could answer, Charlie's glasses were knocked from his head by a school bag slung over the shoulder of a red-haired girl who was passing. She dropped into the seat next to them and rummaged in her bag for her schoolbooks.

"Sorry Charlie, what you two talking about?" she asked without looking up.

Charlie picked up his glasses and put them back on.

"Hi Scarlett, Katelyn was telling me about how we should believe in…"

"Yourself, always believe in yourself, Scarlett!" Katelyn quickly added, remembering something Tilly the Tooth Fairy had told her once.

"Okay," Scarlett intoned, moving her head from one to the other as if to read the real reason on their faces. "Okay, I'll buy it, but I need a receipt."

That was Scarlett Dorsey's famous saying for situations where she knew she would not get the answer she wanted.

Katelyn knew she was off the hook for now.

CHAPTER TWO
Scarlett Dorsey

Scarlett Dorsey was a little older than Katelyn and Charlie, but the three of them had hit it off from the first time they met in the playground. Her hair was dark red and her face was speckled with freckles that stood out against her pale skin, which glowed with a healthy sheen as if it was lit from within. A fact first noted by Katelyn when they met a few years earlier at play, and both knew that they would go on to become best friends.

Her father ran the local corner shop and it was often Scarlett's job to help arrange the morning papers. This had made her an early riser, and she was always up and out of bed just before six in the morning. Katelyn guessed that the catchphrase

Scarlett frequently used had been lifted from him, as she sometimes helped her dad behind the shop counter, meeting and greeting people. Her dad often referred to her as his 'Little Princess', although if anyone else ever said that to her then they had better be very good at running.

"You two do your homework?" she asked and without waiting, carried on. "What did you get for question three?"

Scarlett placed her books on the desk in front of her, pushing Charlie's books to one side. He grabbed them before they fell to the floor and pushed them back into place.

"Homework, what homework?!" asked a startled Katelyn.

"Didn't you do it?" asked Charlie.

"Oh, come on, we had fractions, Katelyn. Thought that was your favourite topic. When did you ever do things by halves?" joked Scarlett and carried on. "Don't worry, it doesn't have to be in till Wednesday. I can help if you are stuck, as long as you tell me the answer to question three?"

"I don't even know what question three is about, I've not even looked at question one or two yet!" Katelyn sighed and put her chin in her hands as if to hold her head in place.

Fraction problems seemed so trivial to her right now as she felt the weight of the fairy world pressing on her shoulders. Time was running out.

"Katelyn, you've been mixing with those tooth fairies too much!" Charlie chirped with a smile.

Katelyn sat bolt upright, and she kicked Charlie under the desk.

"Ouch, what did I do?!"

"Fairies?!" Scarlett's eyebrows shot up.

"Oh no Scarlett, I was just joking with Charlie, that's all," Katelyn felt the room swallow her up.

Scarlett was a good friend but did not suffer fools gladly. She was also the class gossip and news like this would keep the playground going for weeks.

"Come on Katelyn, pass the gravy and spill," Scarlett cast her green eyes over the shrinking Katelyn who was sure someone had turned the heating up and the walls were pressing in on her.

Scarlett over the years had developed her own style of language that she referred to as her 'Street Smarts' which she used to get the information she desired.

She always hoped that in years to come she'd become an investigative reporter such as those that were featured in the morning papers that she helped her dad sell each day in the shop. In her mind's eye, everyone had a story to tell and Katelyn had just become a front-page feature.

"Tell you what, give me dibs on the story and I'll keep it here on the desk for my ears only. We got a deal?" prodded Scarlett eagerly.

Katelyn sighed and resigned herself to the fact that her life story was about to be made the playground story of the week. Maybe by bringing Scarlett into her mission, she could help. If she told herself that enough times, she might just believe it.

Ok, here goes nothing, she thought.

"Scarlett, I've been having adventures with a friend of mine who is a tooth fairy. She collects baby teeth and takes them home to be made into houses for the gnomes, pixies, and...," Katelyn looked at the floor as she talked as if hoping to find a secret escape hatch into which she could jump down, so she was surprised when Scarlett interrupted her.

"Wow..., I did not expect that!" Scarlett exclaimed. "I still have my baby teeth, all of them. Never had a visit from the tooth fairy. Dad tells me it's to do with the fact I don't eat sweets, but I think they are stuck!" Scarlett continued.

"What, really..., but you're like..., nearly ten. A grown-up?!" Charlie looked shocked as he spoke.

"I'm nine still, not double digits yet!" She said sharply.

"A full set of baby teeth though!" Charlie looked aghast at the thought.

"Yeah, read about it in the funny pages, Charlie, it's all true. Look!" Scarlett opened her mouth to show them her teeth.

"Rock solid, not even the school dinners can budge these," she said and tapped them as if to prove their strength.

"How can you have all your baby teeth still, you must have lost at least one?!" Charlie looked astounded as he spoke.

Katelyn looked into Scarlett's mouth as close as she dared.

"They look firm, and they gleam!" she said.

"Told you, still got every single tooth and they're not coming out anytime soon," Scarlett said proudly, tugging on a tooth as if to prove it.

Charlie frowned and seemed lost in his thoughts,

then he turned to his two friends with a grumpy expression.

"When my wobbly tooth comes out, I hope I do better than last time. Would you believe I got a French coin under my pillow…, a franc, can you believe it?" Charlie ranted as his two friends looked on, trying hard not to smile.

"Not like I can even spend it. In France, they use the euro now, got rid of the franc years ago. What do I want with a franc?" he moaned. "It's not like I'm going to France either anytime soon, don't have a passport yet."

Katelyn and Scarlett looked at each other and both of them fell into a fit of giggles.

"Not fair that I don't get a pound, I'm always cleaning my teeth, not fair at all. Just saying!" Charlie finished and folded his arms as he sulked.

By now the classroom had filled up with about thirty children, all scraping desks and dragging chairs into place. The noise was quite deafening, so no one heard the door open to the hallway.

"Settle down children and take your places please, quiet at the back, Larry stop picking your nose and

Cynthia put Andrew down, he's not a toy!"

In strode Mister Walker, Katelyn's teacher. He was a tall man, with grey thinning hair and a habit of wearing red ties and tweed suits, with patches on the sleeves. Katelyn had never seen him outside the school without his tweed suit and tie.

When she thought about it, she had never seen him wear anything but a tweed suit and tie. Maybe that was all he had in his wardrobe.

"Katelyn and Scarlett, stop talking and face front. Charlie Goodman, will you stop prodding your tooth, it will come out when it is ready!" said Mister Walker as he spied a picture that Katelyn had been drawing of him.

"Katelyn, is that what you honestly think I look like?" Mister Walker said, pulling the drawing of himself from amongst a pile of paperwork on Katelyn's desk.

Embarrassed, she sank deeper into her chair.

"Drawing in class is fine during playtime, so long as you combine it with a good education afterwards, which is why we are now starting with history."

Mister Walker strode to the front of the class and turned towards the seated boys and girls.

"Right children, open your textbooks to page fifteen, and who can tell me when the 'Great Fire of London' took place?" he said as he switched on the projector and an image of London on fire appeared on the screen at the front of the room.

Katelyn sat back in her chair and opened her book, although her mind was locked on her conversation with Charlie and Scarlett. How was she going to get people to believe in fairies again if she had trouble getting her friends to understand?

Even she had trouble believing, and she had visited the realm.

Back when she had been given this mission she had been filled with hope and excitement but most people she spoke with treated it as a joke that she had made up to have a bit of fun, but time was running out and no new Tooth Bearer had been found yet to replace her. If only she could get people to believe, to remember, then everything would be alright.

If, and this was a worst-case scenario, no new Tooth Bearer could be found, and she failed to change people's hearts and minds, then the Darkness of Disbelief would spread over all the fairy realm and the inhabitants would be lost.

The fairies once believed that they became gremlins when subjected to the Darkness, but this was false. Made up tales told to the young to get them to go to bed on time. No, the inhabitants became something else, something much worse.

Something Katelyn did not want to meet. She gripped her pencil tightly and buried her face in the textbook. She would not let that happen and would fight tooth and nail to stop it.

As the image on the screen of London burned with the great fire all she could see was the City of Landon, the capital city of the fairies, built with the collected teeth of a generation of humans and shaped not unlike London, being covered in Darkness forever.

No, she would not let that happen...

CHAPTER THREE

Things to do in Haverhill

People in the Suffolk market town of Haverhill would never know of the events that were to take place that night. Most were watching television, safe in their houses, or visiting the pubs and bars.

Certainly, nobody looked towards the medieval church that sat just off the market square with its stone tower that gave a commanding view over the many houses and gardens.

If they had, they might have seen the red eyes glaring at them, huddled amongst the stone gargoyles that graced the top of the tower. Watching for opportunities to unfold, waiting for someone.

The clock chimed eight; the sound echoing around the market square, bouncing off the surrounding buildings like a ball thrown against a wall.

Although a full moon had been predicted, the sky was cloudy, and only now and again would the curtains of the sky part to allow the man in the moon time to gaze at the town. Was it a fearful gaze or a warming gaze, we shall never know.

"So, Uncle Lenny, why do we come up here each night, because I'm getting bored?"

The voice belonged to a small green figure with a reptilian face and two small red eyes that peeped from under bushy eyebrows and a heavy leather hood. Small bat-like wings sprouted from the creature's back, neatly folded. No shoes were worn over his clawed feet. The little figure rested his chin on the stone wall as he stared out over Haverhill with a glum expression fixed on his face.

"Bored, bored, bored!" he moaned.

"Quiet Pichael, tonight could be the night. Watch and learn from your Uncle Lenny," said the other figure who was currently staring at the clouds. He was also of reptilian origin and dressed roughly similarly, with an ill-fitting hood and clothes that seemed to have been taken from a variety of fashions. Odd socks strung alongside multiple old keys hung from his belt.

He smiled a toothy sharp grin at the younger figure, such as a parent might whilst trying to persuade a child that a trip to their great aunt was in their best interest. Rows of sharp teeth, and a few blunt ones, shone in the moonlight from the reptile's mouth.

One, in particular, caught Pichael's attention, for the tooth seemed to be made from a fine crystal that gleamed and sparkled.

"Uncle, when will I get my crystal tooth, so I can use it to travel here and be big, like these statues up here, and...," he thought before continuing, "mess with the human brain?!" he finished.

Lenny frowned at Pichael and leaned on his elbow whilst casually cocking a clawed finger towards the inhabitants of the town.

"We do not mess with the human brain Pichael, we offer a service to keep them on their toes. Stealing car keys, taking odd socks, and hiding them in the cat basket. Putting bright red pants in with a white laundry wash and leaving the fridge door open is all part of what we do. It is not messing but teaching them the facts of life," Lenny grinned revealing a sharp, crystal tooth within his toothy mouth.

"As to your crystal tooth, you get that when you turn eighteen and as you are only eight...,"

"I'm ten, Uncle Lenny."

"Just testing you, okay ten, then you have another five years to wait," Lenny counted his claws slowly as he spoke.

"You mean eight years to wait, Uncle," Pichael sighed.

"Eight, you sure Nephew?"

"Yes, Uncle."

"Well, anyway, you have a few years yet before you get your crystal tooth so stick with me and I'll teach you all I know, just like I taught my best mate Sharpclaw," said Lenny, in his best parental voice.

He let his mind wander as he revisited the past. "We were thick as thieves back then, always fought tooth and claw to get the job done," Lenny smiled again as he spoke remembering his old friend.

"Didn't Mister Sharpclaw get turned to stone?" Pichael asked his uncle.

"Eh, yes he did, but that's not the point."

Pichael slumped onto the floor.

"Why are we here, Uncle?" he asked.

"Well, I received this note telling me to be here when the moon is full and bright, and collect some natural moonlight in this here jar!" said Lenny, producing a crumpled bit of paper and a small green bottle with a cork stopper.

"Don't know who sent it to me, except it's signed with the letter T at the bottom. It said I would get to help an old friend on a secret mission. All for a good cause," Lenny held the note out for Pichael to see.

"What old friend, Uncle?" asked Pichael.

"Well, I've only got a few old friends now. Most I

owe money to so I can rule them out. There is the gremlin ambassador, but I doubt it's him." Lenny's mind wandered as he ticked off people he knew.

"Could be Tiberius, but he's in prison. Sharpclaw is..., well stone last time I looked," pondered Lenny as he screwed up his brow in concentration.

"Sharpclaw starts with an S, Uncle," Pichael sighed and walked glumly to the edge of the tower. "I'm even more bored than a minute ago now. Look at them humans all having fun and I'm not!" he cried.

"You want fun, well ok..., watch this!" and with that Lenny rummaged in a nearby bag and produced a catapult and a small ball. He looked over the town and spied a fat pigeon sitting atop a washing line filled with crisp, clean white sheets.

"There you are, my beauty. Watch this!" said Lenny.

Aiming, he pulled back on the catapult's elastic band and fitted the ball into position, licking his lips he then released the ball which flew straight and fast, hitting the bird squarely in the chest.

'COOOO, SQUAWK', it screamed and pooped all over the clean washing, before flying off.

"Haw, haw, teach'em for leaving their washing out this late!" Lenny rolled around the roof laughing till his sides hurt and his eyes filled with tears.

Meanwhile, Pichael just watched and hid his embarrassment as a teenager might do to a parent that acts silly in front of their friends.

Lenny stopped laughing after about fifteen minutes and looked up from the stone floor where he had fallen over, holding his sides. He sighed and stood up, dusting himself off.

"What's wrong, why can't you be like the other little gremlins?" asked Lenny.

Pichael averted his gaze from his uncle and stared out towards a nearby pub. Some people had emerged and for a moment music filled the air.

"You know, Sharpclaw and I used to get up to all sorts of tricks back in the day. He would have found that a real HOOT, see, pigeon..., HOOT..., get it?" Lenny laughed at his joke but Pichael just sighed again and sat down knowing that he would be in for another fifteen minutes of his uncle's antics. It gave him time to think anyway.

"I miss my dad, Uncle Lenny. It's not fair. Why did he get turned to stone too and end up being placed in a museum by the humans?" Pichael asked.

"Well, you know our fate. If we stay out here in the human realm too long and the golden sun gets us, don't you?" Lenny looked sad for a moment.

"I know Uncle, we end up like these statues here,

and as Mister Sharpclaw did as well," Pichael patted one of the stone gargoyles that sat cold and quiet, guarding the rooftop, the frozen gaze forever locked towards the pub.

"Yes well, Sharpclaw didn't listen to me and with me being the brains of the outfit I was able to escape. Your dad didn't listen to me either, and he stayed out here too long. Wasn't my fault the humans thought he was some ancient stone ornament and carted him off to that old museum basement," Lenny lamented.

"But moonlight brings us back, Uncle Lenny, why not my dad?" asked Pichael.

Lenny screwed up his eyes and wiped his snout.

"You need a full moon, such as tonight is going to be. Plus, your dad has been locked in that old basement for six months. No windows, no moonlight. I'm sorry, that's how it is," Lenny patted his nephew on the head and tried to offer some sympathy. He was not used to this sort of thing, so he tried to change the subject.

"Anyway, you have me now to instruct you and your sister Nancy, talking of which I'd better turn her over or your mum will have my hide for a brand new handbag," Lenny mused as he rummaged in the bag again and produced a large egg which was pale blue, about the size of an adult human head and had green speckles on the shell. Someone had written in ink the name 'Nancy' on the side and had drawn a smiley face next to it.

"Hello Nancy, not long now till Uncle Lenny here gets to show you how to steal socks from the humans, I'm sorry your dad's not here to give you this rite of passage, but I promised your mum and I'll do my best!" Lenny addressed the egg.

"She can't hear you, Uncle Lenny," said Pichael.

"Oh, yes she can, can't you Nancy?" Lenny danced the egg about as one might a baby in the air.

Just then the clouds parted in the sky, and the tower was bathed in rich moonlight. The town clock chimed nine times.

"This is it Pichael, any minute now!" said Lenny as he spun about the tower not knowing quite what to expect.

The moon shone down onto the top of the tower casting shadows all along the rooftops of Haverhill. As the two gremlins stood there a bright light appeared in one corner and got brighter and brighter until they had to shield their eyes and turn their faces away.

The smell of cinnamon filled the air.

"This is it!" he said, just as the light vanished.

CHAPTER FOUR
The Toothsayer...

"There you go Nancy, it's a sign you see, you'll soon be...," Lenny spun back towards where the light had first appeared. His ears pricked up.

"Hope I'm not disturbing you two," said a quiet voice from behind the two gremlins. "I wouldn't want to stop your dancing when you should be working!" the voice snapped.

A tall figure emerged from the shadows of the tower and walked towards the pair, the moonlight casting its gaze briefly upon the face of the new arrival.

"Stone me, I did not expect to see you here, Toothsayer Timoir," said Lenny.

"Who is it, Uncle?" asked Pichael, moving closer to see the cloaked figure who was half-hidden in the shadows. All he could make out was a tall female figure, possibly elderly, holding a staff topped off by a crystal. He thought she might have fairy wings, but he wasn't sure if it was just a trick of the light.

"You found my note…, good, and the bottle is with you as well…, I take it you have it, Lenny?" said the figure.

"Yes, of course, and let me thank you for letting me help you on this mission, Toothsayer," Lenny babbled.

"Speak only when requested," the tall figure rasped as she took the bottle from the gremlin and held it up to the moonlight. She removed the cork stopper and uttered words that the little gremlin Pichael had never heard before.

"Extractus lunacus," she said.

Transfixed, the two gremlins watched as the moonlight streaked down from the sky and bent towards the bottle, pouring itself inside like a mist.

"Uncle, who is that?" asked Pichael.

"That is Toothsayer Timoir. Toothsayer to the Pearly King and Queen of Landon City, and a master mage and advisor at the Ministry of Molars. We should bow," said Lenny in awe.

The tall figure produced another bottle from within the robes of her gown. This one glowed fiery red and burned as if they had bottled the very sun.

"Is the moonlight going to help my old friend Sharpclaw and bring him back, great Toothsayer?" asked Lenny humbly, holding his claws in front of him and bowing on one knee.

"In a way, it will, and in a way, it won't. I will make it a choice for him to make," she said, and opened the fiery red bottle and poured the contents into the now bottled moonlight.

The two ingredients combined into one swirling mix of pale blue and burning red. Cold and hot together as one.

"That's Molten Moonlight, I've read about that in my school books. I thought it was just a fairy tale!" exclaimed Pichael, pointing at the glowing bottle excitedly.

The Toothsayer smiled coldly at the little gremlin.

"When did you learn to read Nephew, and come to think about it, when did you start school?" asked Lenny, giving his nephew a sideways glance.

"Now Lenny, do you know Clare Park?" asked the Toothsayer as she placed the bottle of Molten Moonlight in a pocket within her robes.

"Eh, never met a Clare. Should I know her?" asked a puzzled Lenny.

"It's not a person!" she snapped and took a deep breath, "I did not mean to shout, I apologise," she told the gremlin.

"The town of Clare, which is close to here, has a park with an abandoned train station within its grounds. Make sure you are there on the station platform tomorrow when the clock strikes midnight. I will deliver your friend Sharpclaw to you then," she said. "I will also require you to undertake an important mission for me. You will require these!" she told Lenny.

She rummaged in her long robes and produced a cloth bag full of bright red and white speckled beans, shaped not unlike kidney beans, from her pocket which she presented to Lenny and said, "Do you know what these are?"

"I would say..., a midnight snack?" asked a puzzled Lenny as he examined the beans one by one. He tried to lick one.

"I would not advise eating these. What you hold there are known as Ingress Bloom Beans, otherwise known as Mushroom Fairy Ring beans. Long before we used our magical amulets to transport from our realm to the human realm we used fairy rings that grew in parks and forests from these simple-looking beans," she told the pair as they held the beans up to the moonlight and watched them sparkle as if embedded with hundreds of small magical crystals.

"I need you to plant these beans as you go about your daily routine and create lots of new fairy rings. Plant them wherever you see fit in this world, parks or gardens. I will leave it up to you," she looked sternly at the two gremlins and held up a finger to silence their questions before continuing.

"Do not eat them, they are very rare magical beans and are not your lunch. Now, remember..., be at Clare at midnight on the station platform. Is that clear?" she spoke coldly and her grey eyes seemed to burn into the souls of the two gremlins, making them flinch as they tried to avoid her gaze.

"Very Clare, I mean..., I mean clear, tomorrow at midnight on the station platform at Clare Park," said Lenny, getting very tongue-tied as his legs turned to jelly. He dropped to one knee and pushed Pichael onto his knees as well.

"Do not disappoint me, now if you will excuse me I have business elsewhere to attend to, remember..., do not disappoint me!" growled the Toothsayer slowly as she backed away into the swirling fog of a pale blue and amber smoke that enveloped her in its misty embrace.

Pichael watched the figure disappear. Was it his imagination, or did he see the figure transform into a human as she left, the wings vanishing to be replaced by a red dressing gown?

As the mist cleared, she was gone leaving only the scent of cinnamon in the air.

"Wow!" said Pichael.

Lenny didn't know if Pichael was referring to his lack of understanding of basic instruction, something he had been trying his best at since losing his boss Sharpclaw, or the fact that he had been given an important mission by the Toothsayer. He decided on the second and went with the Toothsayer.

"I know, pretty cool, and you get the smell of cinnamon, two for one…, am I right or am I right!" he quipped.

"So Nephew, all we need to do now is wait for this 'T' person to arrive, and then we can plant mushrooms!" said Lenny, looking over the top of the tower at the people below.

Pichael rolled his eyes and looked sadly at his uncle for he knew that he was being serious.

He sighed and took out a felt tip pen. He drew a picture of the dark figure he had just seen, and the church tower onto the egg shell.

"What are you doing that for?" asked Lenny.

"When Nancy breaks out, she'll need to know what she has missed. So I'm recording everything we do, for her onto her egg. Like a diary," said Pichael.

Lenny looked very puzzled.

"But she won't be able to read when she's born?" questioned Lenny.

"I'll read it to her Uncle!" said Pichael with a sigh.

"Can you read and write then, because I can't?" asked Lenny.

Pichael stopped writing, wondering if he was related to his uncle and not just a mixed-up egg at birth.

You can choose your friends but you can't choose your family, Pichael thought to himself as he held up the large egg. It was warm to the touch and he thought he felt movement.

"I'll show you the world," he said to his sister.

CHAPTER FIVE

An old friend arrives...

Whilst the events on top of Haverhill's church tower were taking place, another figure had emerged into the town.

The smell of cinnamon dispersed into the night and a faint glowing light surrounded the tiny figure that had just appeared dimmed and faded completely, leaving a small girl with fairy wings and pointy ears. She was roughly about two inches tall and wearing handmade clothes with a tin hat made from an old bent Saint Jude medal on her head with the letter 'T' inscribed onto it at the front.

Her skin shone and sparkled in the moonlight and was quite pale, with a slight silver sheen to it that contrasted against her large bright green eyes.

She tucked a lock of bright red hair, which had fallen out-of-place, back amongst the curly green hair that sprouted unevenly beneath her tin helmet and cupped a crystal necklace that hung around her neck in her hands, so that the light that was dispersing from it could be hidden from view.

"Let's not wake the neighbour's cats and dogs!" she said to herself as she placed the necklace under her tunic. It felt warm next to her skin as the light faded.

She adjusted her clothes and looked around the area. She knew the garden well from the many visits over the years. It hadn't changed much.

She was a tooth fairy and had collected the baby teeth from this house for many years now. She always requested this collection even before she had known the little girl that lived here.

She breathed in the air and smiled. This felt like her second home these days.

Looking through the bushes that grew around the edge of the garden, she checked for birds that might see her as a midnight snack.

A giant pigeon landed in the middle of the lawn looking for fallen bread, and she quickly opened the bag that was slung around her shoulder.

She slowly withdrew a small needle that she used

as a sword and clasped it in front of her.

"Thimbles and needles, will you fly away?!" she shouted at the bird who just looked at her. She noticed that the bird looked as if it had been punched in the stomach by something. A small, metal pellet fell from its feathers onto the ground.

She pulled out a bent pin that was tied to some dental floss. Usually, this would help snag hard to reach teeth that had been placed under a sleeping child's pillow, however today she found another use for it as she spied some stale bread on the lawn, and waving the pin around her head by the floss she threw it towards the crumb, and on the third attempt snagged it on the pin.

Pulling hard, she pulled the bread towards her before the bird could see what was going on.

"Okay Walter, or whatever your name is, go get this!" and she threw the bread with all her might over the fence into the neighbour's garden. The bird followed, giving her the chance to slip out from the bushes and fly across the lawn to the house where an upstairs window had been conveniently left open.

She peeped through to see a young girl sitting cross-legged on the bed wearing a white top and pink trousers. She had blonde hair that stretched down her back and freckles around her nose, one freckle, in particular, was shaped like a heart. An expectant smile was plastered on her face as she waited for her friend to arrive.

"Hello Katelyn, here I am!" the softly spoken tooth fairy said as she entered the room.

"Tilly you made it, goodness I was getting worried you wouldn't come tonight!" said Katelyn to her friend.

"Wouldn't miss it for the world, nearly your birthday and miss a party…, never!" said Tilly.

"You know I'll always try to get here, even if a pigeon tries to stop me. How are you?" Tilly asked.

"Fine, thank you. Come in and sit on the bed."

"I've got some milk and cookies for the birthday feast," Katelyn said as she placed a plate of chocolate chip cookies on the bed. "I've been doing some drawing whilst I waited for you."

She held up a picture of Tilly that she had just finished.

Tilly

by Katelyn Flowden

"That's very good, I like how you have done my hair," remarked Tilly.

"Have you collected many teeth tonight?" Katelyn asked the little fairy as they both sat together on the bed and started eating.

"Actually, only about seven. It is quite quiet these days. Although I have been asked by the Ministry of Molars to keep an eye on this red-headed girl who still has all her own baby teeth, and would you believe, is nearly ten!" Tilly exclaimed as she held a cookie in both hands.

"That will be my friend Scarlett Dorsey, I bet. I'm meeting her at the park tomorrow. Why don't you come along as well?" Katelyn clapped her hands together as the idea of introducing Tilly to her friend formed in her head.

"Well..., let's not rush things just yet, I am only supposed to watch over this Scarlett Dorsey, not go for a chat and a picnic!" Tilly shrugged her shoulders as she spoke. "However, I will be in the area. The gnomes at the Royal Exchange are anxious that if all her teeth come out at once they will need to issue a cheque for a lot of money, instead of just the usual coin. So I have been told to be her extra shadow and monitor her," Tilly spoke with a frown. "I can't believe they want me to babysit her," she said.

"I really don't think Scarlett will want her baby teeth coming out in one go. How would she eat?" Katelyn thought out loud. "Anyway, they are as hard as nails. Not even the school sponge pudding can budge them," Katelyn laughed as she thought of her friend.

"They do seem that way," said Tilly and as she munched on a piece of cookie. Suddenly she had an idea and with a beaming smile jumped up. "Katelyn, as it is nearly your birthday, I think we should go out and have some fun tonight!" Tilly smiled as she spoke through the cookie crumbs.

"Fun, go out, what..., really?" asked Katelyn, jumping up from the bed.

"I know someone who has lost their tooth and is expecting a visit from a tooth fairy tonight. Would you like to watch?" asked Tilly.

"Really, be a tooth fairy and collect a tooth, yes please!" said an excited Katelyn.

"Watch a tooth fairy, Katelyn," reminded Tilly. "The fairy is an old friend of mine, she lives in the City of Light and I don't get to see her very often. In fact, she collected one of your teeth before I got the contract here," continued Tilly happily.

"How will I be able to watch, I'm big, aren't I?" asked Katelyn.

"That's easy, the crystal I gave you, it's..., let's see..., it's beside your bed next to your lamp!" Tilly glanced around the room and finally pointed to the clear-cut transparent crystal that sat beside the lamp. About three inches in height, it shone with many varied colours as the lamplight caught its sharp sides and projected a sparkle effect of red, green, and blue light onto the wall as if a party was taking place.

It was used to communicate with Tilly whenever either of them wanted to talk to each other. Easier and cheaper than a phone call and like a mobile phone it could fit inside your pocket and didn't require a contract. Perfect for any little girl's needs when talking to magical fairies!

Katelyn had also been gifted with a magical school satchel embossed with her initials on the front. It was made from the same material as the sack that presents were carried in by Father Christmas and it could hold any amount of items that its owner placed inside, which admittedly were usually collected teeth and money when a tooth fairy used it.

As it was now in Katelyn's possession however it held many small toys and collectables that she had found in her room, plus the odd chocolate chip cookie.

They also gave her a tin hat that resembled the helmet worn by Tilly. This one had the letter K written on the front, and she was very proud of this.

Tilly smiled and said, "The crystal has the power to shrink you to my size. We can watch the collection and be back before your parents come to check on you."

"After the last time I don't know…, something always seems to go wrong and I don't want to end up your size Tilly. I've got some new school clothes and my parents will climb the walls if I cannot fit into them because I'm only two inches tall!" Katelyn worriedly exclaimed.

"Don't worry, I'll make sure everything is fine, trust me!" Tilly grabbed Katelyn's hand.

"Alright, it sounds fun, but I must tell my mum and dad where I am going. They would be ever so scared if I'm missing!" Katelyn exclaimed.

Katelyn loved the little fairy with all of her heart and knew that Tilly would look after her always. She was known as a careful tooth fairy that had carved out her career in the tooth collection business after leaving the family home many, many years ago to live with her Aunt in the city.

"Deal, I am sure they will say that it is fine, they know me," agreed Tilly.

Neither Katelyn nor Tilly even considered the fact that most, if not all parents, would utter a resounding 'NO' to the fact that their child had asked if it was alright to go outside with a friend at that time of night. However, in Katelyn's eyes, if you didn't ask, you didn't get!

"How will this work Tilly, it's not as though I can just fly into someone's house?" asked a bemused Katelyn flapping her arms about as if flying.

"Okay, press the crystal against the palm of your hand and think of something small, like a grain of sand," Tilly said, showing to Katelyn the technique.

"How about I think of you, Tilly?" laughed Katelyn.

"Hilarious smarty pants, I'll have you know I am considered quite tall for a fairy!" retorted Tilly with a smile and carried on, "I will fly you to my friend and we can watch the collection..., easy."

"The crystal won't break like your necklace did when I first met you, will it?" a worried Katelyn suddenly asked, remembering how she had initially ended up in the fairy realm after accidentally touching the necklace that hung around the fairy's neck as Tilly had prepared to depart.

"This crystal is bigger and designed especially for you. When you return you just place your hand on the crystal and think of something large, like a mouse or a cat and 'POOF'..., normal size again!" Tilly said confidently.

"Okay, but first I had better pack something for the flight," said Katelyn placing some cookies inside her satchel and grabbing her helmet from the hook on the door where it hung at the ready for adventure.

"These chocolate chip and cinnamon cookies are really nice, but I'd better not eat too many or I'll be collecting my own teeth soon," joked Tilly eating another and sniffing the air to take in the sweet smell that she knew so well.

"Didn't know I'd bought cinnamon cookies, but save one for me, Tilly," Katelyn said as she opened her bedroom door and headed out to find her parents.

Closing the door she turned around to the staircase and suddenly jumped with shock, having not seen the figure, dressed in a red dressing gown that was standing, hidden in the shadows.

"Oh..., hello Mummy, I was just coming to see you. You gave me a fright!" Katelyn said in a shocked voice as she caught her breath.

"Hello Katelyn, are you ready for bed yet?" her mum said. In her hand, she held a small box wrapped in tissue paper and tied with a bow.

"Mummy, my friend Tilly the fairy has come to visit and wants to know if I can go and visit another fairy and collect a tooth..., please can I? Pretty please with sugar on top? I can wash dishes for a month. Can I go with her?" pleaded Katelyn, clasping her hands together.

"Well, it isn't a school night and I guess the fairy will look after you. Tilly, you say?" asked her mum.

"Yes, you know Tilly. I promise I won't be long and I'm so excited. It will be brilliant, please can I go Mummy?" by now Katelyn was jumping from one foot to another foot and holding her hands together as if praying.

"Just remember what make-believe is and what isn't. It's fun to have imaginary friends and real ones," said her mum.

"Make believe?" said Katelyn to herself.

"Half an hour, then bed!" replied her mum.

"By the way, Katelyn, I had hoped to give you an early birthday present. I know it's still a few weeks away, but I wanted you to have this now. It is very special and quite old," her mum presented the box to Katelyn who grasped it lovingly. Wrapped in red tissue paper with a blue bow, it looked very beautiful.

"Thank you so much, Mummy, what is it?" she asked excitedly.

"Wait and see. Why not put the box beside your bed and open it in the morning, then it will be more of a surprise? Have fun and don't be too long, Little

Miss."

"Brilliant, you are the best mum in the world. I promise we won't be long. I love your glowing makeup, by the way, you'll have to show me how you do it when I get back!"

Her mum silently watched Katelyn rush back inside her bedroom and shut the door behind her. Turning around, she starred into a nearby mirror that hung on the landing wall and touched her face.

"I don't see any glow?" she said to herself.

She ran her hand down her cheek before sliding over to the closed bedroom door and pressed an ear against the wood to listen. She smiled to herself as she heard the conversation within.

"Mummy said I could go, and she gave me a present, aren't I lucky!" Katelyn said excitedly to the little fairy as she placed the parcel carefully beside her bed, ready to be opened the next day.

"What is it, aren't you going to open it?" asked Tilly.

"When I get back!" said Katelyn, her face frowned suddenly as she thought about her mum's conversation earlier.

"It was strange as if she didn't know you."

"Adults find it hard to hold onto the magic and are quicker than most to forget our realm. That's why your mission is so critical to us," replied Tilly.

"I guess so," said Katelyn, looking sad.

"Cheer up, adventure awaits. Now put on a coat, it is freezing outside!" laughed Tilly.

Katelyn looked around her room and quickly pulled on a pink, sleeveless, body warmer style jacket.

"Aren't you in the pink!" laughed Tilly.

"Mummy bought it for me, it's very warm. Just the thing for collecting teeth," remarked Katelyn, buttoning up the jacket.

"Observing!" stated Tilly.

"Yes, that as well," Katelyn remarked, clearly not listening.

"Let's go!" she said excitedly to her fairy friend.

"Okay, now place your hand on the crystal," said Tilly, which Katelyn did, and the very next second she stared into the smiling, silvery face and large green eyes of her old friend. Katelyn always liked the fairy wings that protruded like fine lace from her friend's back. The detail on them was exquisite.

They hugged each other warmly.

"Wow, it worked. I'm really tiny again!" said the little girl, jumping from one foot to another. Her little tin helmet bobbing up and down on her head.

"Well, I'd say you were the right size but come on, take my hand and off we go!" Tilly grabbed her friend's hand and pulled her into the air. Up they flew through the room and out of the open window, into the evening night's moonlit sky.

"Don't let me drop, please don't let me drop!" cried Katelyn feeling a mixture of wonder, excitement, and fear. She didn't know which emotion to feel first as they were all pushing to be number one.

"Well I haven't lost anyone yet but I guess there is always a first time...," laughed Tilly.

"Excuse me!" shouted a shocked Katelyn.

"Ha, ha. Don't worry and hold tight. I'm joking, I won't let you fall!" laughed Tilly, her eyes sparkling.

Katelyn closed her eyes and felt the rush of the cool night air blow across her face. She opened one eye slowly and looked down across the town. There was the church and the local library where she had spent many a Sunday as part of a book club.

It all looked so small, like a model toy town. Katelyn expected to see a little train come shooting out of a shoebox tunnel someplace.

She looked across at Tilly the Tooth Fairy and squeezed her hand just as the moonlight shone down through the clouds and lit up the wings of the little fairy, making them glow with a pale blue aura as they beat the air with a speed that made them almost invisible to the naked eye, propelling them upward into the sky. It was all so exciting.

Outside on the landing, Katelyn's mum nodded to herself as the sound of her daughter drifted away.

"Didn't see you come up here, I thought you were asleep on the sofa still, are you okay?" said a voice behind Katelyn's mum. She spun around to see a man standing on the stairs behind her in his dressing gown and slippers. He looked tired.

"I'm fine, I've just put Katelyn to bed so please be quiet. I've got a bit of a headache right now, general tiredness I think..., parent stuff. Would you fetch me a glass of water from the kitchen, please?" she asked sweetly.

"Sure, rest, and I'll bring some up," said the man heading back downstairs, his slippers flapping on the staircase as he trudged back down.

"Like the new dressing gown!" he said as he went.

The woman watched him go before smiling a faint, crooked, uneasy smile as if the upward movement of the sides of her mouth were new to her.

Clicking her fingers, she made clouds of pale blue and amber smoke appear that enveloped her torso in the cool misty embrace that folded about her body like a coiled snake trapping their prey.

As the smoke disappeared she was gone as if she had never existed, except for a slightly sweet smell of cinnamon that hung in the air, until that slowly vanished as well and silence filled the room once more.

Meanwhile, downstairs, Katelyn's dad was pouring out some water when he suddenly said to himself.

"You know, I bet some cinnamon toast would go

down a treat with this water..."

"Cinnamon toast?!" asked Katelyn's mum coming into the kitchen holding an empty glass and rubbing sleep from her eyes.

"Why did you change your dressing gown to a blue one? I liked the red one," he said.

"Red one?" said the woman, but the conversation was cut short by an alarm going off.

Beep, beep, beep.

"Who on earth set the smoke alarm off!" she said.

CHAPTER SIX
Meeting Mariel

As the little girl and her fairy friend sped upwards through the night, hand in hand, Katelyn thought she heard an alarm ringing out from her house, but that noise was soon drowned out in the rush of air as she flew higher and higher over the rooftops.

"Don't let go!" shouted Katelyn as she tightly gripped the hand of her tooth fairy friend Tilly.

Tilly's wings beat a hundredfold as she powered through the night. You could hardly see the little delicate lace wings that sprouted from Tilly's back as she flew against the moonlight, creating an aura of pale blue light that emanated around the couple.

"You're doing great, Katelyn, look down there!"

Tilly pointed towards a nearby garden as they descended.

Down they went into a steep curve, aiming for the house and garden.

"Wheee!" they shouted together, joyfully.

At the last moment, Tilly slowed her wings and righted herself, bringing the pair to a controlled stop at the garden's edge and landing in some soft moss.

"There, how was that Katelyn?" Tilly asked as she dusted herself down.

"That was great, I thought I'd be scared flying like that but I wasn't!" Katelyn exclaimed happily.

"We'd better watch out for cats and dogs, remember...," started Tilly as she peered around the well-kept lawn.

"A careful tooth fairy is an extracted tooth fairy," finished Katelyn with a smirk.

"Okay, smarty pants. Let's go, it seems safe enough," said the little fairy as she took Katelyn's hand and led her towards the house.

"This place sure looks familiar, whose tooth are we after tonight?" asked Katelyn as she stared at the very large house.

"Well, strictly speaking, it's not us that will do the collecting. I've been asked to have a word by the Ministry of Molars with...," Tilly wasn't able to finish her sentence for suddenly another tooth fairy flew down at speed, hit the ground, and completed a forward roll that finished up directly in front of the two observers.

The new little fairy sat on the ground and looked up at the startled pair. She had a shoulder bag slung around her neck and a quickly dimming pendant that Katelyn easily recognised for it was identical to Tilly's.

On her head, she wore a red felt beret hat. Her face was quite round and she was shorter than Tilly. Her hair was bright orange and red, and very windswept from the flight. She wore a little jacket, a skirt, and purple and red stockings that finished in painted acorn crafted clogs. She blinked and smiled before jumping up with an outstretched hand.

"Bonsoir Miss Tilly, comment allez vous?" she said, grasping Tilly's hand and shaking it vigorously.

"Hello Mariel, I am fine, thank you. Let me introduce my friend. This is Katelyn, the Tooth Bearer," Tilly said as she nudged Katelyn forward.

"Oh, I'm sorry I don't speak French, Mariel," said Katelyn as she shook the hand of the new fairy.

"That is not to worry, I will speak the English, Miss Katelyn. I see you have grown a lot since I last collected a tooth from you. How old are you now, twelve?" asked Mariel.

"Nearly nine actually. I remember you left me a note in French," responded Katelyn happily.

"Tout à fait, just before Tilly got the job, and I returned to my beloved City of Light," Mariel attempted to sort her hair out with a comb as she talked. "The curse of the long-distance tooth fairy, I cannot do a thing with it," she moaned as she gave up with her hair, then she smiled at the pair.

"So Miss Tilly, what brings you to this garden?" she asked.

"Well, I thought it would be nice to bring Katelyn along as a treat to see a professional at work. It's good to see you again, Mariel. Did your Republic

Exchange tell you to use a franc again?" asked Tilly, as she spied the coin in Mariel's bag.

"Of course they did, it is a good coin, non?" Mariel replied.

"Mariel, France uses another coin now, it's called the euro. Why are you giving Charlie a French coin anyway, the Republic Exchange should give you the right coin for the country beforehand, shouldn't they?" Tilly carried on.

"Oui, they should, and they should also tell people it's not just little mice collecting the teeth as well, but they don't...," began Mariel.

"I can see you dressed as a little mouse!" laughed Tilly.

"La Petite Souris is a tradition in France, it takes years to train the mice to collect baby teeth. You can never remove the smell of cheese from your clothes though!" said Mariel frowning.

"Rather Brie than me!" laughed Tilly.

Engrossed in their conversation, Tilly and Mariel failed to notice that Katelyn had ventured closer to the house.

"This is Charlie's. I thought I knew this house!" interrupted Katelyn, spinning around to look at the building. She noticed a light had come on inside.

"Charlie's family originally came from Lyon in France, Miss Tilly. They are homesick. The coin is but a simple reminder..., I guess. So what harm is there in that?" asked Mariel.

"Well, none, when you put it like that. However, it's not like Charlie can spend his franc on anything here?" said Tilly.

"Oui, I know. I'd happily give a pound from my purse if I had one. Our Republic Exchange gives us the coin and we take the tooth. I will not question their reasons for giving me a franc instead of a pound. I am sure Charlie likes the reminder of his home country," replied Mariel.

"Well, to be honest, I don't think Charlie has ever been to France, or anywhere else, come to think of it...," began Katelyn.

"It seems our Exchanges, both Royal and Republic aren't talking to each other again," said Tilly.

"The gnomes that run the Exchanges are so grumpy. Always thinking that they know what is best for the children. They never ask us!" said Mariel. "It is an Exchange issue and both sides, Republic and Royal, will sort it out between themselves. Let the gnomes argue about the red tape, not us!" she said.

"I agree. Our Royal Exchange tried to hand out a

shilling the other day that they found down the back of a sofa," replied Tilly thoughtfully.

"So different cities in your world have their own types of Exchange, for handing out the coins and taking the teeth?" asked Katelyn.

"Oui Miss Katelyn, the City of Light, where I come from, has the Republic Exchange and Miss Tilly here, has to deal with the gnomes of the Royal Exchange in Landon City," answered Mariel.

"Wouldn't it be easier to just have the one Exchange, swapping a tooth for a coin?" questioned Katelyn.

"One Exchange? The gnomes would never go for that!" stated Tilly.

"Non, non, non, the gnomes love their red tape. What would they argue about if there was only one Exchange?" Mariel genuinely seemed shocked at the very idea.

"Which gnome spent the least coin and filed the most forms, wasn't there an old poem about it?" laughed Tilly.

As the little group chatted amongst themselves a door on the house opened, and a silhouetted figure could be seen standing there holding a torch.

"They do love their paperwork. I do recall that old

verse," Mariel paused for a moment as she tried to remember how it went before continuing.

"Give a gnome red tape and files,

And you've got a gnome that smiles,

Take away his things to do,

And you've got a gnome that's...,"

"Full of p...," interrupted a giggling Tilly.

"GRUMPY AT YOU, Tilly, honestly!" Mariel quickly finished her poem.

"Guys, we may have a problem!" said Katelyn in a small scared voice.

Neither Tilly nor Mariel heard her though or noticed the large human shape approaching.

"Let us put the problems with the Exchange and their squabbling gnomes behind us?" asked Tilly.

"Oui, I agree..., Oh no!" said Mariel as a bright beam of light illuminated the area where they stood. Three little faces stared upwards at the source.

"Fairies in my garden. Katelyn was right, after all, I do believe, I really do!" said the tall, unmistakable shape of a human as it loomed overhead.

"Oh boy, here we go again...," groaned Tilly.

CHAPTER SEVEN
Here we go again...

"Fairies in my garden, I can't wait to tell Kate...,"

"Hello Charlie, fancy seeing you here," said the little girl that stood between her two fairy friends, all of them shifting nervously from foot to foot as if they had been summoned to the headmaster's office.

"Katelyn..., KATELYN, you're a little fairy!" Charlie stumbled over in his slippers and dressing gown and fell with a thump on the lawn. As he went down, his torch flew off into some nearby bushes and landed on the ground amongst some red and white mushrooms.

"Katelyn, I can't believe my eyes, I must be asleep and dreaming, is it..., is it really you?!" he stammered, fumbling around in the dark on his hands and knees as he looked for his torch.

"Non, non. Ne le laisse pas toucher ça... I mean, don't let him touch that!" shouted Mariel quickly.

"Charlie, STOP!" shouted Katelyn with all the air that was in her little lungs.

Charlie stopped his hand just inches from the ring of bright red and white mushrooms that sprouted from the ground at the bottom of the garden. His face was pale in the moonlight and he was visibly shaken.

"Step away from the mushrooms!" commanded Mariel as best she could, considering she was only about two inches tall.

"What is going on, I need my teddy!" said Charlie, huddling up and sucking his thumb.

"Charlie, it's alright. Everything is going to be alright," said Tilly as she flew over and put a comforting hand on his shoulder.

"Charlie, it is me!" said Katelyn, running over to where he sat against a nearby tree.

"Katelyn, I don't know what to say. You're so small and you're a fairy!" Charlie took a deep breath to calm down as he stared at his little friend. "Have you come for my tooth?" he asked.

"Well, sort of. Do you remember what I spoke to you about in school earlier, well it's all true. This is Tilly and Mariel and they are both tooth fairies and friends of mine," Katelyn waved her arm towards the other two.

Tilly flew up and hovered in the air, taking a bow in front of Charlie. "Hello," she said.

"Bonsoir Charlie, je m'appelle Mariel," said the other fairy as she did a little curtsey on the ground.

"Hello everyone," said Charlie weakly.

"Charlie, are you alright?" asked Katelyn.

"Are you a tooth fairy, Katelyn?" asked the little boy who was still shaking, but by now that was because he was outside in his dressing gown and slippers and it was quite cold.

"No, not at all. I just came along for the ride tonight. I don't have any wings, see!" laughed Katelyn as she showed Charlie her back.

"Excusez-moi!" shouted Mariel, motioning for everyone to come over to her.

"Mariel, what is it?" asked Tilly as she flew over towards the mushrooms and her friend.

"Look at these, do you recognise them? See how the spots glow in the moonlight?" Mariel asked.

"It's a mushroom fairy ring!" said Tilly excitedly.

"Oui, you are quite right, Miss Tilly. However, these are known as Ingress Bloom mushrooms. Do you remember your history lessons and the rhyme that we were all told when young?" Mariel asked Tilly.

"Well, I could do with a refresher course," said Tilly shuffling her feet.

> "Grown in glade by brook or tree,
>
> Fairy rings just for thee,
>
> Step within by moon's first light,
>
> To be taken against your might!"

Mariel announced to all then she examined the mushrooms carefully, with Tilly looking over her shoulder.

"It is most odd, you see these crystals embedded in the mushroom skin. That is not natural at all!" Mariel exclaimed in astonishment.

"They look like miniature Seeing Stone fragments!" said Tilly as she peered closely at one fungus.

"Why would someone wish to create a hybrid ring,

it is most strange?!" pondered a curious Mariel.

"Where is my torch, I can't find it? Last I saw was when it fell into the mushroom ring!" moaned Charlie.

"Your torch, young Charlie, is gone. It has been whisked away to our realm and I know not where!" Mariel looked anxious.

"Mariel, what's wrong!" asked Tilly looking anxious as she saw her friend's pale face.

"This is old fairy magic, before our time. They used these mushroom rings, before our pendants, to travel from our world to here and back. Trouble was you could never judge exactly where the magic would take you." Mariel frowned as she explained.

"It was all very random and you could end up someplace you didn't want to be. Humans would sometimes accidentally walk through a fairy ring and we'd have to bring them back home if we could find them," said Mariel in an anxious tone.

"So if Charlie had fallen inside this ring he'd be in our land someplace, and we'd have no way of knowing where he ended up," said Tilly.

"Oui Miss Tilly, and unless there is a ring on the other side to get you back, he might be stuck. A little giant in a little land. Not good, not good at all," sighed Mariel.

"Giant..., but when I visited I was the size of a fairy?" asked Katelyn.

"It was my talisman that made you small when you first visited. Fairy ring's just drop you, full size in our land. People used to think fairies captured humans that fell into the rings!" laughed Tilly.

"Who planted them here?" asked Katelyn.

"That is a good question. Only the Ministry of Molars has access to these magic beans, and they wouldn't let just anyone have them," replied Mariel.

"I think I need to speak with our Toothsayer. I bet Timoir will know more about them," said Tilly thoughtfully.

"First though, let us get young Charlie here back to his bed and collect his tooth. He has had a busy night indeed," Mariel said to the group.

"Am I going to get a French coin again?" asked Charlie, somewhat glumly but trying not to sound ungrateful at the same time.

Mariel slipped the French franc she had half produced back inside her bag and rummaged about.

"Non, not this time Master Charlie. You should have this crystal, it is a Seeing Stone," she said as she produced a large crystal, shaped like a rough triangle, from her bag and pressed it into the little boy's hand. The sides were smooth and from deep within the frosted mineral, a dim, pulsing glow of bright white light could be seen.

"Wow, I have one of those as well. They are really cool Charlie. You can call any fairy you want to for a chat, like a free mobile phone, but without your parents worrying," said Katelyn to her giant friend excitedly.

"Oui, when you need us just call out our name into the crystal, and we shall find you," Mariel said in her best instructor voice.

"Well Katelyn, looks like your recruitment drive is working!" said Tilly with a smile.

The group made their way back to the house and into Charlie's bedroom to retrieve the tooth, but not before Charlie had carefully kicked over the magic fairy ring to prevent others from falling into it.

As it was cold, and to avoid unnecessary explanations with Charlie's parents if they met them, the trio of little people climbed into Charlie's dressing gown pocket to keep warm and hidden.

Katelyn had never ridden in a dressing gown pocket before, but she found it very warm and cosy, not unlike being wrapped up in a warm bed with the sheets over your head. A nice, safe feeling.

As they walked, she wondered where the torch had ended up and if they would ever see it again. It had been a busy evening and by now her parents would be anxious. They made it to the bedroom without interruption, thankfully.

"Goodnight Charlie, if you are at the park tomorrow I'll see you there around eleven?" she said to her friend as Charlie climbed into his bed.

"Okay Katelyn, I'm sure this is a dream but I hope it isn't. Goodnight Tilly, goodnight Mariel," he responded and was soon sound asleep.

"Fais de beaux rêves," said Mariel as the trio went outside.

"Sweet dreams," echoed Tilly.

"Well, I must return to my city and deposit this tooth. Take care you two and beware of those fairy rings, I sense foul play at hand. We must report it at once. Please let me know if you find anything!" Mariel said to the pair as she prepared to depart.

"We will. Take care and keep in touch Mariel," said Tilly.

"I will. Now both of you, be very careful. Au revoir," she waved goodbye and gave each of them a hug. A brilliant bright light emanated from the pendant she wore around her neck and enveloped her until all that the pair could see was a faint silhouette within. As the glow vanished the familiar smell of cinnamon remained in the air and the little fairy in the beret had vanished.

"Come on Katelyn, I better get you home before you fall asleep on me," said Tilly.

"I can hardly keep my eyes open, can we call a taxi?" asked Katelyn.

"That won't work, I don't carry any money for tips, just teeth. It's not far and I'll have you home in the time it takes to clean your teeth," the little fairy said as she took Katelyn's hand in hers and the pair lifted off the ground and flew back home.

By the time Tilly had returned Katelyn to her normal size and tucked her into her bed, she was fast asleep. The wrapped present from her mum would have to wait till the morning.

"Goodnight my friend, sleep well," she said to the sleeping girl. She held her necklace and the now-familiar bright light and smell of cinnamon filled the room before she too was gone.

Elsewhere, in another land and on another world, a desert stretched out as far as the eye could see. The sand was dry and fine, like the flour that a cake is made with.

It was so fine in fact that were you to stand still in the sand you would sink through it and never be seen again. The only way to survive was to keep moving and never stop until you made it to solid ground, not even for a moment.

It was known as the Desert of Lost Wisdom because only a fool would travel there and it ran alongside the Enamel Coast where the last bastion of civilisation sat before the endless sea stretched out into the distance. An area that most, if not all, people tried to avoid.

A strange tower made of metal stood upright in the sandy dunes, the base wedged between a small group of rocks.

A bright glow shone out of the top, straight up into the night's sky that created a cone of light as if to illuminate the millions of stars in the sky that looked down upon this strange structure.

It looked like a lighthouse, except where a door might have been there was a small panel held tightly shut by a single metal screw and inscribed with the words 'MEGA-BRITE' in neon red. Two small rubber buttons sat above the lettering marked ON and OFF. The only other feature was a name written above the panel in white paint.

It read 'CHARLIE'.

On the distant horizon, a strange shape approached the tower from the south, gliding over the sandy dunes with an almost stately grace, like a ballet dancer leaping across the dance floor.

A sailing ship of some sort, perhaps?

The vessel resembled a sixteenth-century sailing galleon that had been combined with a steam engine, coupled with an airship. At the front sat a huge wooden figurehead of a black raven, the wings stretched tightly around the bow like a hand protecting the craft. In the middle of the deck rose a large brass funnel that was connected to a steam boiler that spewed smoke into the sky and provided the power for the two rear-mounted fan blades that propelled the strange ship forward.

On the port and starboard sides of the craft, which were the left and right-hand sides, sat two long wooden beams with cotton sails attached that protruded horizontally out into the desert and helped steer the vessel, whilst navigating over the top of the dunes.

Finally, attached high above the craft, there hung a large, well-patched balloon made of silk and lined with paper that kept the ship aloft and safe from sinking into the sand.

The traditional skull and crossbones symbol, favoured by all pirates, adorned the front of the balloon.

Two figures stood at the bow of the craft.

"Better wake the Cap'n," said one, a tall, thin sprite.

"He won't like it, he needs his beauty sleep. Never likes it if he doesn't get his full eight hours, Mister Carver," said the other, a waif-like female fairy wearing a bandana.

"Wake the Cap'n, now Janice!" said Mister Carver.

The female fairy headed off slowly into the craft, only to return with an even shorter figure wearing a nightshirt. He was a gnome with heavy, bushy eyebrows and carrying a large brass telescope.

"Well, well, well. Now you don't see that every day, do you lads?" he said with a gruff, harsh voice.

The owner of the gruff voice lowered his old brass telescope slowly from his eye and folded it away.

"Mister Carver set a course for that there metal lighthouse, full steam ahead!"

"Aye, Aye Cap'n, full steam it is!" replied the tall sprite behind the owner of the gruff voice.

"Haw, haw," the gruff voice laughed.

"Unusual to have a lighthouse in the middle of a desert, what say you, Mister Carver?"

"Very unusual Cap'n, ain't no rocks round here big enough to break yer keel," replied the tall figure as he raised a short brass telescope to his eye.

"It seems to have a name on it, Cap'n. It reads 'CHARLIE'. Perhaps this Charlie is at home and has some booty that he'd like to lighten his load with?"

"Capital idea Mister Carver, let us acquaint ourselves with the owner."

The ship slowly turned towards the metal tower, and as it did, the sun picked out a brass name plate bolted behind the figurehead.

It read 'THE RAVEN'.

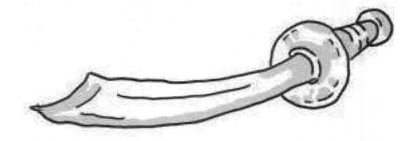

CHAPTER EIGHT

Between a rock and a hard place...

Whilst Tilly was tucking Katelyn back into bed, events were unfolding in the capital city of the fairies.

Influenced heavily by the architecture of the human cities, the City of Landon sat on two sides of a long winding river, looking very similar to a certain human city on which they had designed it. Both cities had palaces, bridges spanning the river, places of industry and commerce. In fact, they were almost mirror images of each other except for the fact that the fairy city was built using the collected baby teeth of many a child. This had been proven to be a very versatile building material. Hard-wearing and with a brilliant shine made keeping the city gleaming a straightforward task.

The Pearly King and Queen had ruled over the city as was tradition and were well respected by the community. King Stepney and his wife Queen Clement had lived at the Crystal Palace ever since the previous sovereign, King Pontin, had disappeared to the country around nine years previously. Or that's what the fairies thought. Rumours persisted about an attempt to stop the blight that infected the land that failed dismally.

Close to the Crystal Palace was the famous Royal Exchange. Run by the gnomes, this was where the tooth fairies would deliver the retrieved baby teeth and collect the coins that would be placed under the pillows of the many sleeping children of the human realm.

The tall, grey monolithic spire known as the Crystal Shard, where the ceremony to force back the Darkness of Disbelief took place, dominated the centre of the city, and was surrounded by market stalls of every shape and size. All selling their wares from the four corners of the world to the population.

Here the baby teeth of a Tooth Bearer would be locked into many circular brass rings that surrounded a giant Seeing Stone crystal. The power channelled through the teeth and into the huge crystal would, for a time being at least, hold back the Darkness of Disbelief until a new Tooth Bearer could be found, and the process renewed.

Close to the river, about a mile from the Crystal Shard was an imposing building known as The Ministry of Molars. They constructed it over many levels and it housed the lodgings of the senior magic-user and advisor to the King and Queen known as the Toothsayer. Currently, this position was held by the fairy known as Timoir.

The building also served as a school to hundreds of tooth fairies in training and as a centre point of magical studies for the fairies, sprites, and pixies that lived there. Gnomes never touched magic, preferring rather to tinker with machines or read up on the latest modern invention.

Finally, at the very edge of the city was the famous Tower of Landon. Constructed in a similar style to the human version, this was also a huge four-tower structure that housed the City Guard and the prison.

Crime was very rare in the city, but just lately events had occurred that warranted building such a place. That said, the rooms, as they were never called cells, had been nicely decorated by one of its new occupants, the royal painter known as Tiberius Smart. He was a flamboyant gnome, ever quick to tell of his brilliance, and with an equally cavalier dress sense. His clothes were as colourful as his painted portraits. Many of the Kings and Queens of the realm and Tooth Bearers' past had been immortalised in his oil paintings.

However, he had tried and failed to prevent the Tooth Bearer ceremony from taking place and was now serving his time decorating and repainting the Palace and surrounding buildings.

As he sat, writing in his journal by candlelight he thought he heard movement on the other side of his door. He paused briefly, his quill hovering over the page. "Must be hearing things, Tiberius," he said to himself and carried on writing.

Nobody saw the tall female figure move silently and slowly, wearing a red dressing gown and looking very much like a human..., but looks can be quite deceptive, as this was no ordinary human.

She entered an open chamber where, in the centre, stood a stone statue of a gremlin which the figure stood staring at for a moment, as if in contemplation of her forthcoming actions.

She moved her hand across her face and as she did a glowing light followed it. The figure grew wings and transformed into a tall, dark hooded fairy. In her hand, she held a staff, topped by a shining crystal.

She withdrew the heavy black hood and revealed a

familiar visage, for it was the face of the city's Toothsayer, known to many as Toothsayer Timoir. She smiled to herself as she looked upon the cold stone character that stood before her.

Walking towards the statue she removed a warm, glowing, corked bottle from a shoulder bag, and opening it she poured half the contents over the statue. As the hot, sticky liquid seeped into the stone cracks, she uttered an incantation.

"What was once stone be flesh once more. Let moonlight caress and soothe the jaw. Let limbs be free and eyes let see the dawn of day on this stone set free."

She stood back and observed her work. The lines and cracks in the statue pulsed with an orange light that made it look as if the rock was lit from within, not unlike a volcano that spews lines of red, hot lava from its depths.

The light got brighter and brighter, to the point where she had to shield her eyes. A final blast of brilliant, bright orange light shot out of every stone joint and illuminated the entire room until the very statue itself could not be seen. Even with her hands over her eyes, the orange light was unbearable and she had to turn her head.

After a short time, the glow faded and standing there before her stood a gremlin. It staggered forward and stumbling, fell to one knee.

The creature looked up at the figure that stood before it and smiled, revealing a mouth full of razor-sharp teeth. Its eyes narrowed as it tried to focus.

It tried to speak but could only manage a guttural, low growl that sounded like sections of a cliff face falling and smashing into the sea below.

"Welcome back to the realm gremlin, or should I say Sharpclaw?" hissed the Toothsayer coldly.

The cold red eyes of the gremlin stared back at the Fairy. An audible hiss was heard from its throat.

CHAPTER NINE
Sharpclaw again!

"The petrification effects will wear off in a minute. Rest for a moment, try not to talk," said the Toothsayer in a cold, commanding voice.

"Where am I?" asked the gremlin as he slowly regained his voice.

"You are in a cellar in the Tower of Landon. You can thank me for freeing you, Sharpclaw," she responded.

"Sharpclaw again, Stoneclaw no more, as it should be. So what name do I give to my saviour then?" the gremlin snarled. "What KIND person would wish to free old Sharpclaw from his stone prison, and why?" he looked up slowly and nearly fell over backwards.

"Toothsayer Timoir, the last fairy I expected to see. Even that little girl, Cake Tin, or whatever her name was. The one who set me here in these stone shackles. Yes, her I would expect to free me. For she had a good heart, or that Tilly fairy, one with the silly hat. Yeah, she might free me if conscience pricked her side," he snarled.

"Not you though, your heart was stone long before mine ever was!" Sharpclaw spat out each word, in his venom-filled hatred of the Toothsayer.

"Have you finished dear?" asked the fairy.

"I've got an entire book of terrible words I'd like to call you, Fairy," he waved his fist at Timoir and noticed for the first time since being set free that he could move his claws.

"Happy?" asked the Toothsayer.

"My claws! I forgot what it was like to have this fist. Guess I should thank you, Tim…," he stopped in mid-sentence as he starred at Timoir. "Wait a minute. Show yourself Timoir. Your true self, not your false image. I know glamour magic when I see it!" he accused the Fairy, stepping forward menacingly.

"Of course my dear, you deserve that much at the very least," the Toothsayer said sweetly and crept her hand across her face. A glow followed her hand as her features changed.

"Apart from a few extra lines and wrinkles, you look the same. Are you sure your spell worked?" queried the gremlin, as the fairy revealed her true self.

The figure before the gremlin had a pale almost silver complexion with a hook nose and a thin mouth. Although she looked very old she resonated strength, power, and authority. Her robes were of the deepest darkest purple with a dark wool wrap that covered her shoulders. On her head, she wore a twisting conical, deep purple hat that spiralled upwards like a snake.

"I am known as Toothsayer Tiana, and I was once the Toothsayer to the great King Pontin. I have freed you from your stone prison because I have a job offer for you," Tiana said sharply.

"I already work for Tiberius, don't need another boss. Ta anyway and thanks for freeing me, I'll be off then..., cheers," Sharpclaw walked towards the exit but was stopped in his tracks.

"When I said I had an offer, I meant I had an offer that you couldn't and shouldn't refuse," said the Toothsayer in a cold harsh voice. "You see this potion I used on you, it's called Molten Moonlight. Now, ordinary bottled Moonlight would free you without question, but Molten Moonlight is a little different," she said casually.

"You have my attention it would seem," Sharpclaw said as he stopped walking and turned around to face Tiana.

"Good, well as I was saying, Molten Moonlight requires the whole bottle to free a petrified person and I seem to have only used half. Now, it's called Molten Moonlight because it is rather like hot lava mixed with moonlight. If the treatment isn't fulfilled within a certain amount of time by using the whole bottle then, well..., I think you know what happens to lava when it cools?" she looked at the gremlin sternly and spoke with a slightly crooked smile.

"...," said Sharpclaw.

"Indeed, dear, back you go to being a rather lovely garden ornament," Tiana said happily.

"Not all bad news though, it will protect you from those harmful human sun rays. Stops you from turning all concrete on me. Works a bit like sun cream really," she added with a smile.

"It would seem that I have a new boss then," Sharpclaw's shoulders fell as he spoke, for he knew there was no escape.

"Oh, goody. I'm glad you've come round to my way

of thinking, Sharpclaw. We are going to be such good friends. When this is all done I promise to let you have the rest of this potion. Pinkie promise," she said brightly, which unnerved the gremlin, for he felt as if he were a mouse caught by a playful cat.

Sharpclaw glared at the fairy.

"Follow me, my dear Sharpclaw, for we have some teeth to collect," and with that, she moved her hand across her face once more and replaced her image with that of Timoir the Toothsayer.

The pair easily moved across the city, keeping to the shadows and staying out of sight. Nobody would question the motives of Toothsayer Timoir, such was the respect the folk had for her and Sharpclaw kept himself hidden under the heavy hood worn originally by Tiana.

They soon stood outside the enormous tower known as The Crystal Shard. The heavy wooden doors were locked shut by eight strong metal clasps.

"Well, when you said you were going tooth collecting, I thought you meant teeth still stuck in human heads. Not Tooth Bearer teeth. Didn't you read about Tiberius's failed plot last year?" Sharpclaw joked. "Don't want to mess with the Tooth Bearer, that girl has got a mean set of weapons up her sleeve. Her fault I was a statue in the first place. If I ever see that Cake Tin again I'll…, I'll give her a piece of my mind, that's for sure!" he ranted.

"Don't give her too much or you'll have none left!"

"What?!" blurted Sharpclaw.

"Be quiet, we will deal with the Tooth Bearer after this, now watch and learn," Tiana said as she stretched out her right arm. A long thin bone wand slipped into her palm from within the sleeve of her robe.

Pointing the wand at the sealed clasps on the wooden door, she uttered the magic words "open up!"

Sharpclaw stood open-mouthed.

"Open up, OPEN UP…, is that it, no fancy words or dancing around the courtyard?!" Sharpclaw mocked the magic user, but as he finished a bright blue light shot out of the wand and hit the metal clasps holding the door shut. They flew apart one by one like a flowing wave until the door stood open. Cold air rushed out to greet them.

"Why use six words when two will do," said Tiana as she replaced her wand inside her sleeve. The pair headed up the steps into the first chamber.

The room was circular, with grey rock walls that had small chips of rock crystal entombed within. These occasionally lit up with a faint blue light as the pair passed, which provided the only light source within. Two stone staircases snaked up to the next floor.

"Get the teeth and be quick, for we shall soon have guests. Do as I say and only as I say," Tiana commanded.

Sharpclaw looked about the room and saw small red flashing lights strung about the ceiling.

"Oh, rookie mistake. Tripped the fairy lights did we?" Sharpclaw laughed to himself as he headed up the staircase at a brisk pace to the room above.

"Halt, you are under arrest for trespassing on property of the crown," said a loud voice behind Tiana. She turned slowly to see six Royal guardsmen, a mixture of fairies, sprites, and pixies all armed with short swords. The officer in charge stepped forward, holding his short sword out in front of him.

"Halt I say, by order of Captain Tyler of the Royal Guard!" the officer commanded.

"Oh, Captain Tyler, So nice to see you again," responded Tiana sweetly, as she removed her heavy hood whilst still disguised as Timoir.

"Toothsayer Timoir, so sorry ma'am. Did not know it was you," said the officer as he quickly saluted and sheathed his sword.

"Can't be too careful ma'am, had trouble around here in the past, as you know only too well!" the Captain continued.

"Yes, it is good to know that the Royal Guard is always on hand to spot any wrongdoings going on," replied the Toothsayer.

Just then Sharpclaw came back down the stairs clutching a bag. He wandered casually over to the Toothsayer with the sack slung over his shoulder. He hadn't noticed the group of guards who now stood open-mouthed at the sight of the notorious gremlin thief.

"Had a spot of bother prizing the teeth free. Luckily, my claws are sharp. Like home-grown lock picks, these things are. Could've used your wand back there, Twinkle toes, and that open spell of yours, but I got the job done as you asked," he said as he arrived beside the Toothsayer.

"Hey, aren't you Stoneclaw the Gremlin? How did you get free?" Captain Tyler shouted as he quickly drew his sword again.

"Captain, he's got the Tooth Bearer teeth in the sack, I can hear them rattling, and look, I can even see one in there!" said one guard, quickly pushing forward to stand beside his captain.

"What, open that sack this minute, by order of...," shouted the Captain so loudly he attracted a small crowd of locals who were walking past. They stopped to see what all the fuss was about.

Sharpclaw sneered and interrupted by saying, "Yes, I know how it goes. By order of Captain so and so of the Royal Guard, and for your information, my name is Sharpclaw!" He flashed his claws at the guards as if to emphasize his name. The crowd looked shocked and took a step back almost in unison as fear overcame them at the gremlin's  name being mentioned. Whispering and muttering could be heard as the crowd backed away.

A short fairy in a flower printed dress stood amongst the crowd holding a wax basket full of shopping that she was taking back home. Her name was Pippa Sevenpenny, and she knew the real Toothsayer Timoir from previous adventures.

She squinted hard at the Toothsayer before her. Although it was dark and her eyesight wasn't what it used to be she could easily make out her friend, but there was something odd about her this time, that she just couldn't put her finger on.

She tried to call out to Timoir, but her throat dried up when she witnessed the Toothsayer take out what looked like a handful of small red-coloured beans and throw them at the feet of the Royal Guardsmen. Suddenly, from the ground around the guard's feet sprang red mushrooms, speckled with many fine crystals and white spots.

The mushrooms grew instantly into a ring that surrounded the Captain and his men and in a sudden flash of light, the guards had all vanished.

The Toothsayer turned to the crowd and took a small bow before saying in a loud voice "Ladies and gentleman, fairy folk and all. I bid you a fond farewell, for I have a date with a Tooth Bearer and a train to catch!"

With that she grabbed the gremlin and his sack of teeth and touching the necklace that hung around her neck she vanished in a flash, leaving only the smell of cinnamon to linger on the breeze and a stunned Pippa Sevenpenny, standing wide-eyed and open-mouthed in the dimming light. The crowd almost as one took a step back as the figures departed the area but Pippa stepped forward. Her face had become a frown.

"Something is not right, not right at all!"

CHAPTER TEN

That's not my fairy...

"I don't believe it, Timoir would never steal the Tooth Bearer teeth, and make Captain Tyler vanish like that!" Pippa said aloud to anyone who cared to listen, then added, "Well, maybe make the Captain vanish if he annoyed her, but not steal the teeth."

She looked around the open courtyard where more and more fairies, sprites, pixies, and gnomes were gathering. Each had the same stunned expression locked onto their face. A group of constables had arrived as well and had begun taking statements from the witnesses.

"I need to find Tilly, she'll know what's going on," and with that, she picked up her wax basket and headed into the Crystal Shard tower. If she could reach the giant Seeing Stone within the tower she could ask it where Tilly was. As she wasn't a tooth fairy or a mage, she didn't possess a magic necklace or talisman, so had to rely on her wits to gain information. The constables had already begun roping off the area inside, but she slipped up the stairs unnoticed.

The giant Seeing Stone on the second level was just the same as the one that Katelyn and her friend Charlie owned, except this one was ten times larger and pulsed with a faster white light. Surrounding it should have been the collected Tooth Bearer teeth. Now, however, only the empty brass holders remained. Broken padlocks lay strewn around the floor, each of them covered in heavy scratch marks.

She stood before the stone and pressed the palm of her hand against the crystal. She thought of her niece, Tilly Lightfeather, the red lock of hair that always protruded from her tin hat, her green eyes, and the way she smiled. Nothing seemed to happen, though.

"Come on, where is she?" she asked herself.

"Excuse me, should you be here?" asked a female constable as she came up the stairs.

"Oh, sorry. I seem to have mislaid my keys, I know I had them earlier, I'm such a flutter brain," Pippa began kicking the dust around in an attempt to trace the non-existent key.

The constable walked over to where Pippa had crawled around in the dust. She looked up at the uniformed figure before her and saw that she was a gnome, slightly taller than most, with steel-grey eyes and a strange glimmer of light around her face.

Suddenly the gnome transformed before Pippa's eyes and grew to become a tall fairy with fine lace-like wings, lines and wrinkles crossed the face, yet the steel-grey eyes had a twinkle of an adventurous youth long ago.

"Toothsayer Timoir, am I glad to see you. I'm guessing you didn't steal the teeth and send the guards to goodness knows where then?" Pippa said sharply as she got up off the floor and dusted herself down.

"Of course not Pippa, although making some individuals disappear has crossed my mind from time to time. I can assure you it wasn't me. As soon as I heard that the fairy lights had been set off I came down here as fast as I could. Sadly not fast enough to stop that imposter," Timoir calmly said.

"Don't know how you can be so calm Timoir, someone is pretending to be you and causing a right cavity in the tooth. They freed that Stoneclaw as well," said Pippa in an agitated voice as if she expected the gremlin to jump out.

"As I can see, by these broken padlocks and scratch marks," said Timoir as she inspected the debris around the room. "So whoever freed the gremlin knew that magical wards protected these padlocks and only brute force and ignorance would free them, otherwise they'd have used an unbarred spell."

"She also used Ingress Bloom mushrooms to make the guards vanish, I haven't seen that fungi since I was a young fairy," said Pippa.

"I am impressed Pippa Sevenpenny on your

knowledge of mushrooms. They are indeed very rare, only a top-level mage would be allowed to have access to those beans these days," said Timoir.

"Well, I do run the Mushroom Inn. Anyway I am trying to get hold of Tilly and I thought I'd try to use this large crystal, but it's about as much use as a toothless gnome in an apple-bobbing competition," said the irate fairy.

"You need to be a mage to use this Seeing Stone," said the Toothsayer, who seemed lost in thought as to who could have done this deed.

"Well?" said Pippa, indicating the crystal with her thumb.

The Toothsayer held out her palm to the crystal and said in a commanding voice, "Show me where Tilly Lightfeather is!"

Almost immediately an image formed within the crystal and the familiar shape of Tilly the Tooth Fairy appeared. She seemed to be in a bank.

"That's the Royal Exchange, come on let's go!" Pippa said excitedly as she grabbed and pulled Timoir along by the hand.

"Wait Pippa, right now a lot of the city thinks I am a criminal. Allow me to change if you will?" and with that Timoir passed her hand over her face.

Pippa watched as the body of the fairy shrunk, and the wings pulled in and disappeared. The shoulders became more rounded as did the face. Once again the female constable stood before Pippa. The pair hurried out of the Crystal Shard as fast as they could.

Outside an immense crowd had gathered around the entrance and Pippa and Timoir had no trouble in mixing with the throng of sprites and fairies, pixies and gnomes that milled around. They hurried through the streets passing street vendors selling newspapers proclaiming that the Toothsayer had betrayed the city and stolen the Tooth Bearer teeth. That Sharpclaw also was free again, and that anyone with any information on the whereabouts of Captain Tyler and his men should report it immediately.

"This is not good, not good at all," said Pippa as she bought a copy of a paper entitled 'The Fairy Tales Gazette' from a vendor and started reading it.

"As long as we don't panic we shall be alright," said Timoir in an unusual gruff gnome-like voice.

"Yes, of course. I just noticed that Martha Flitwick, owner of the Rested Sprite Inn, was offering a buy one, get a one-night free offer. That woman will put us all out of business," Pippa glared angrily at the paper before tucking it into her wax basket.

"Yes, I can see how pressing a problem that is. Anyway, here we are," said Timoir heading up the ornate enamel steps to the large wooden double doors that would open into the entrance foyer of the Royal Exchange. It was a large circular building decorated with many designs of gnomes and fairies delivering coins and teeth.

White enamel pillars lined the foyer, holding up the high stone ceiling with a central round crystal dome that allowed the room to be filled with natural light. On sunny days, the enamel floor gleamed.

On one side were high booths of dark wood where gnomes sat counting out coins for teeth. Dark wood bookcases that extended nearly to the roof contained ledgers of every tooth collected. The name of the child and age when the tooth was delivered was all entered in meticulous detail into the books by the gnomes who worked day and night.

A fresh addition to the Royal Exchange was a Nectar Tea Expresso Shop, and this is where the duo found Tilly sitting eating a cake.

"Tilly, there you are. Have you seen the news?" asked a puffed-out Pippa rushing up to her niece.

"Aunt Pippa, what are you doing here?" asked Tilly through a mouthful of lemon cake as she quickly tried to remove as many crumbs as she could.

"Oh, hello Constable, is everything alright?" Tilly said, slightly shocked when she saw the uniformed gnome that arrived with Pippa.

"Have you finally arrested my aunt?"

"Tilly Lightfeather, honestly!" exclaimed Pippa.

"Tilly this is Toothsayer Timoir in disguise, we have a real problem on our hands!" Pippa said a little too loudly considering the building echoed, and it carried her voice around the room.

The gnomes huddled behind desks and booths, the tooth fairies dropping off teeth, and just about everyone else, all stopped what they were doing and looked up at the trio.

A silence filled the room.

"Well, if we wished to make an entrance, that's the way to do it!" said the constable.

The gnome passed her hand across her wrinkled face and immediately grew into the Toothsayer once more.

"Hello Tilly, it is so nice to see you again," said the Toothsayer to Tilly, who immediately dropped to one knee out of respect for the elder fairy.

"Please, stand. We are not on ceremony today and I have no time for formality," said the Toothsayer to Tilly.

Tilly stood up and straightened out her tunic.

"Toothsayer, I am glad you are here. I really should have tried to get an audience with you earlier. You see, I met up with an old friend, a fairy called Mariel from the City of Light," she started to explain.

"We discovered a strange fairy ring of mushrooms growing in a child's garden that she said was old fairy magic and that they were dangerous and should never be touched!"

The Toothsayer held up her hand for Tilly to stop talking. "Slow down, Tilly," she said.

"Let me guess, they were Ingress Bloom mushrooms, and when something entered the ring it disappeared?" asked the Toothsayer.

"Yes, that's what Mariel called them. The little boy dropped his torch into the ring when he saw us and it vanished...," Tilly stopped talking as she realised what she had said.

"When he saw you?" asked Pippa.

"Well, you see he was a friend of Katelyn the Tooth Bearer, and I thought that she could go with me to collect his tooth as it is her birthday soon and I...," she faltered as she talked.

Her inner brain was shouting at her to stop talking as the hole she had begun to dig was now getting much deeper and even her wings wouldn't be able to fly her out.

"I think I messed up again, didn't I?" she asked.

"Well, it is true that we want humans to believe in us again. However, it is the Tooth Bearer's mission to do that and not yours Tilly," said Timoir. "That said you have brought me some very interesting information that ties into recent events here. Those same mushrooms were used at the Crystal Shard earlier to make a group of guards vanish as well," pondered the Toothsayer.

"Ingress Bloom Beans grow quickly into fairy rings, however the ones I saw earlier sprang from the ground like rockets taking off!" Pippa stated as she waved her arms about as if to demonstrate.

"I'm confused, did someone plant them here then?" Tilly questioned her Aunt.

"I saw Timoir, I mean someone dressed like Timoir, throw the beans at the guard's feet, and up they sprouted. The guard's never had a chance. She then caught a train," proclaimed Pippa.

"What, where would they vanish to?" Tilly took a step backwards, nearly tripping over the table she had been sitting at.

"Fairy rings planted in the human realm bring you here, so a fairy ring planted here would send you to the human realm. Where you would end up though, is a random event," said Timoir as she pondered what Pippa had said.

"Someone is doing some aggressive gardening!" said Tilly as she mulled over everything she had heard from her friends.

Toothsayer Timoir who had been reflecting on the events sat down in a chair, she felt drained of energy.

"Pippa, you said she caught a train?" asked Timoir.

"Well, she said she had to catch a train before she vanished!" replied Pippa.

"Catch a train, that's an odd thing to say!" said Tilly.

"She mentioned the Tooth Bearer as well!" Pippa said to Tilly.

"Katelyn, what does she want with Katelyn?"

"I need to go to her!" said Tilly, fearful for her friend as she pulled out her talisman from beneath her tunic and prepared to leave.

"Tilly, wait. You don't know what danger you are flying into!" said the Toothsayer.

Timoir was silent for a moment as she thought, then she looked up at the other two.

"It seems these mushrooms have been laced with

an extreme growth potion that causes them to grow instantly. Potions and spells only a high-level mage would know. If the fairy rings are growing in the human realm, as Tilly has witnessed, then we have a much bigger problem on our hands than I previously thought," said the Toothsayer.

"I cannot believe the fairy ring discovered in this human child's garden is a one-off event," she said, and her shoulders fell as if the weight of the world had been placed upon them. Her face was very grey. Tilly and Pippa exchanged worried glances.

"If other rings are growing in the human realm, then anyone who steps within their circle would be transported to our world. They might already be here!" a shocked Pippa stated.

"Aunt Pippa, you said someone that looked like Timoir threw these beans, what did you mean?" asked Tilly who also had to sit down.

Timoir was the first to answer the question.

"Glamour magic Tilly, a spell that alters people's perception of a person, it masks their original appearance. I used it to become a gnome earlier. Any level three mage can do it," said Timoir from her chair.

Pippa nodded her head and exclaimed "I thought it was that. It explains the glimmer around the face you sometimes get when you see them up close!"

"All this happened whilst I was sitting here eating cake. What else have I missed?" Tilly asked Pippa.

"Tilly, you must have heard what is going on. The Tooth Bearer teeth have been stolen from the Crystal Shard and Sharpclaw has been freed. Someone is pretending to be Timoir and...," Pippa suddenly stopped as she noticed a group of Royal Guardsmen enter the building.

Timoir suddenly looked a lot older. She spoke quietly when she said, "I have my suspicions who it is, but it can't be her, it can't be. I think I need to speak with our old friend Tiberius!"

"Oh my, I think we've been rumbled!" Pippa said as the guards marched over to the trio.

They look serious!" said Tilly, as she pointed at the approaching guards.

"Toothsayer Timoir, by order of the King we need you to come with us. Please hand over your wand and talisman."

"You are to be confined to your quarters pending the investigation by order of King Stepney," said the officer in charge.

Tilly pointed at Timoir and said to the officer, "How can you, she is the King's Toothsayer!"

"Orders are orders, I'm afraid," said the officer.

CHAPTER ELEVEN
Timoir in chains

Timoir squinted at the officer as he approached. He was a Pixie and wore the regimental insignia of the King's own guard on his red and gold uniform. He was slight of frame and looked as if he had pulled the short straw with this assignment as he moved awkwardly towards the Toothsayer.

"Captain Shaw, isn't it?" as she looked over towards the approaching guards. "I remember your grandparents being in the guards when I was a tooth fairy, many moons ago," Timoir addressed the Officer who bowed out of respect.

"Yes Toothsayer, I wish the circumstances were better in which we could meet," he said with authority, however, Timoir noticed that he was looking more at his feet than her.

"As do I. You have nothing to fear from me. If I must, I will comply with your request," said the Toothsayer and she handed over her magical items, albeit somewhat reluctantly. She turned to Tilly and Pippa, who were standing behind, watching with open mouths.

"I trust you, and I need you to trust me. I will talk with the King and Queen. It is better to sort this matter out now than to run. However, Pippa does your hotel have a, I believe you call it, a computer?" asked Timoir.

"Yes, it's all-new, though I'm still learning. I'm already on the social sites, though. Have you seen my Fairy Book site, I have lots of followers. I do all my invoices and take bookings for the hotel, and...," started Pippa excitedly.

Timoir interrupted quickly, "Good, then please order one of those fairy doors as quickly as you can, and have it delivered to the Tooth Bearer's house. I worry that Katelyn may be in danger, and without my talisman, I cannot help her directly," she handed Pippa a piece of paper that she had written instructions upon.

"Any particular brand, I've seen a nice wooden one with flowers and a little light that...," Pippa was distracted again by the excitement of shopping.

"Pippa, please. I don't mind about the brand. Just get it to Katelyn quickly. Tilly, please go to her as soon as you can. I will do what I can from here as soon as I have spoken with his Majesty."

"I don't know for sure, but I have my fears about who is responsible. Someone I'd feared long lost may well be coming back to taunt me. I must speak with the King if he'll see me, but we must hurry or I fear it will be too late," Timoir placed her hands on the shoulders of Tilly and Pippa.

"Trust me and it will be alright," and with that, she turned and walked towards the guards and said, "Alright, let us depart Captain."

Once Timoir and the guards had gone Pippa and Tilly left the Royal Exchange and ran through the streets as fast as they could to The Mushroom Inn. They were both out of puff when they arrived. Pippa had run the inn, which was shaped like a mushroom with a thatched roof, for many years. Tilly had worked and lived at the inn for several years as well when she left home, before enrolling at the Ministry of Molars to become an official tooth fairy.

"I wish your necklace could just zap us here instead of all this running about," puffed Pippa as she held onto the front door handle for support.

"Auntie, you know how it goes. It only works to the

human world and back," wheezed Tilly as she held her sides. "We ran and flew as fast as we could!"

"I'm just saying life would be easier on my feet and wings," Pippa said as she staggered through the door and motioned for her two staff members to come over.

"Florence, Dexter, please stop what you're doing and log me onto my computer quickly, and bring up the shopping page please," shouted Pippa as she rushed through to the office.

"I thought you said you know how to do it, Aunt Pippa?" said Tilly.

"I do, I just ask Florence or Dexter!" she retorted.

Dexter brought through some nectar tea to drink whilst Florence set up the computer and logged Pippa in.

"Look at this, all fake news for sure!" said Florence.

A social media site entitled 'Believe it First' was ablaze with news and comments, claiming that in America there was a resident by the name of Mister Baum of the State of Kansas who had seen a group of uniformed fairies all armed with swords, that he thought was an advance guard of an impending invasion force. They were flying about his prairie farm and complaining that they had a feeling they weren't in Landon anymore.

The pair soon found a site selling the fairy doors in hundreds of different shapes, sizes, and colours. Over the years they had become quite fashionable with the humans as home and garden decorations.

"That one is nice, it has a little letterbox as well," said Pippa as she pointed to a little green door.

"I don't think it matters, so long as they can deliver it today. Order it, Aunt Pippa, please," replied Tilly.

"It's done, the order is on its way, Tilly. Now save Katelyn before it is too late and I'll make sure that Toothsayer Timoir is alright," and with that, the smell of cinnamon filled the air and the room was lit by a bright light. Tilly had left the building.

CHAPTER TWELVE
The walls have ears

Katelyn opened her eyes and yawned as the morning sun streamed through the open curtains. Her window was slightly ajar and a warm breeze blew through into her room. As she lay there, she wondered if last night had been nothing but a dream. Had Tilly visited her and taken her out into the night, flying through the air?

She swung her legs off her bed and sat there blinking for a minute or two as her sleepy brain tried to catch up with the rest of her body. Her toes edged their way around her bed until they found her slippers and she reached for a cup of water, hoping that the refreshing drink might wake her up, but her sleepy fingers instead discovered the present that her mother had given her the night

111

before, still wrapped up beside her bed.

Katelyn, like any other child, loved presents and quickly tore off the paper to reveal a long slender golden box which, upon opening held a beautiful dark rock, almost as black as the night and ever so slightly polished, yet it still retained the feeling that it had been just carved out of the earth. It was suspended on a fine silver chain so that it could be worn around the neck.

She sat for a moment admiring the gift, allowing the sun to touch the dark sides of the rock and tried to put it around her neck, but her fingers stumbled on the clasp.

"Mum, can you help me with my beautiful necklace please, I love it!" she shouted at the top of her voice, as most children do when they want the attention of a parent. Downstairs she heard her parents talking and then the click of a door closing. Jumping up, she rushed to the window and stopped suddenly, for there on the back lawn was a large fairy ring of eight or nine red mushrooms with white spots.

It hadn't been a dream after all.

She rushed into her parents' bedroom and peeped out of their window. There she saw her mum heading down the path towards the town. She took a step back in shock, for from this window, which overlooked a large open grassy area, could be seen five or six large fairy rings. All with the now-familiar red and white spotted mushrooms.

"Oh, no!" she said as the thought of her mum accidentally stepping into one of those rings on her way to the town and being magically transported to goodness knows where filled her mind with fear.

She quickly got dressed and pulled on a bright yellow hoodie to keep warm and headed downstairs. Her dad was eating breakfast at the table when she entered the living room.

"Dad, where is Mum going?" she asked quickly.

"She's off to get some new batteries for the smoke alarm. It made a right old racket last night. I'm surprised it didn't wake you!" he laughed, and carried on talking. "I like that new fancy necklace you're holding. It looks like it's made of Whitby Jet. May I see it, please?"

Katelyn quickly passed him the present she'd received and ran for the front door. Flinging it open she rushed down the path expecting to see her mum disappear in a flash, never to be seen again.

"Mum, don't step in any fairy rings!" she shouted at the top of her voice just as the neighbours came out of their house next door. They were an old couple and had lived there for many years. They seemed troubled by something as they kept entering and leaving their house.

"Hello, is everything alright?" asked Katelyn politely.

The wife looked up as if she had been searching for something just as the husband went back inside.

"Katelyn, hello dear. If you see our cat Pebbles on your travels can you send him home please?" she said as she scanned the horizon for the lost cat. "We put him out last night, as usual, and he seems to have slipped his collar again. He does like to forage, and I don't want him eating any of those mushrooms he keeps insisting on playing around with. Thank you, Katelyn," said the neighbour and went back inside.

"I'll do my best," said Katelyn feebly, knowing full well what had happened to Pebbles. She stood for a while staring at the fairy rings. They looked so pretty with their red tops and white spots as if they had been pulled straight from a fairy tale book.

Which, in a way, they had.

Meanwhile, back in the front room, Katelyn's dad was examining the necklace in the morning light, turning it this way and that and holding it up to catch the sun reflecting on its surface.

"I'm sure it's Whitby Jet. Wonder where she got it?" he said to himself, turning the necklace around in his hand. As he rubbed the smooth surface of the black stone, the rock disintegrated into a thick, dark black cloud that enveloped him. He fell, fast asleep, into a nearby chair.

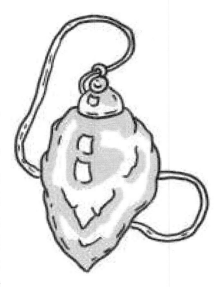

"Did you mean that to happen, or are you just making it up as you go along?" quipped a reptilian voice from the shadows of the front room.

"I admit I had hoped the Tooth Bearer would be snoring by now instead of this bumbling buffoon. However, not to worry. A good fairy always thinks on their wings. I shall prevail!" and with that, the tall shape of Toothsayer Tiana emerged gracefully from a wall, like a ghost, and behind her, the shorter, green-skinned gremlin known as Sharpclaw followed.

As they emerged through the wall, the colours and textures of the surface pulled and ran off the pair like wet paint, spilling and mixing in an artist's palette and sprung back into place. The plaster surface rippled finally like a pond and became solid once more. The Toothsayer waved her wand at the wall and placed it in her sleeve.

"That hiding in a wall spell is a neat trick Tiana, wish you'd teach it to me. Could pinch loads of things if I could just sit on a wall and pop out on the humans whenever I liked. Think of the fun I could have!"

joked Sharpclaw as mischievous thoughts formed in his brain.

"You will call me Toothsayer Tiana, and I am not about to teach you the Cavity spell. Remember your position in this arrangement, I lead and you follow," retorted Tiana.

"Alright, keep your wings in place, I ain't forgot about your Molten Moonlight potion. You just keep your end of the bargain, okay?" said Sharpclaw with a snort.

"Agreed, I am glad we are on the same page," smiled Tiana as she moved into the room.

The Toothsayer moved her hand over her face and transformed into Katelyn's mum whilst Sharpclaw rummaged through the belongings of the household. He came across a fashion magazine and opened it at the male adult fashion section.

"How come we are human size now?" he said as he flipped through pages of suits and ties.

"Because I'd hardly be intimidating if I was only two inches tall. Humans don't have the greatest hearing and I'm not going to risk losing my voice having to shout at them," Tiana replied sharply.

"Well, how about you glamour me up as well and make me look like this?" he said, pointing with a claw at the open fashion magazine.

"You want to look like a man standing in his underpants staring at the horizon?" asked Tiana.

"What..., NO, this page with the man in the dark glasses wearing a suit!" blurted Sharpclaw as he quickly flicked through the pages of the magazine.

Tiana looked up suddenly and shoved Sharpclaw against the wall. "Conceal obfuscate," she chanted as the gremlin fell through the surface of the wall, to be hidden within.

Tiana slid her hand across her face casting a glamour spell, her wings faded from view, and the tips of her ears smoothed to form the rounded shape of human ears. She took on the form of the mother of Katelyn once more and quickly adjusted her hair.

Rolling her jaw as if she had eaten some food that had become stuck in her teeth she said, "I don't think I'll ever get used to being a human, it feels so limiting. How does one fly in this realm?"

"They use aeroplanes you know, flying machines, that sort of thing. Then charge money for the joy of it!" said the wall, where once Sharpclaw had stood.

"I see, how sad for them to not have wings," said Tiana as she pushed her now human jaw into place as the spell took hold fully.

"Now be silent, our guest has returned."

CHAPTER THIRTEEN
The fairy door

The front room door opened and in trudged Katelyn, looking very anxious, with the weight of the world on her shoulders holding her down.

"Hello dear, what's wrong?" asked the disguised Tiana, trying her best to sound compassionate.

"Mum, you're back. I thought you went to the town for batteries?" Katelyn took a step backwards in shock. Her eyes were wide at the vision before her.

Something was wrong. Her dad was asleep in the chair and the far wall seemed to move slightly as if alive. The room scared her.

"Well, I'm back again. Do you want some breakfast, we could make pancakes if you like?" her mum asked.

"Did you get the torch batteries then?" Katelyn asked as she hastened over to where her dad slept in the chair. She tried to wake him by shaking his arm, but nothing would rouse the sleeping dad.

"Of course I did. The torch is ready to go. Now, how about those pancakes? Shall we make them together like we used to?" asked Katelyn's mum.

"Ha, I caught you out!" snapped Katelyn, spinning around to face the disguised figure of her mum. "You went out for smoke alarm batteries, not torch batteries. Who are you really and what have you done to my dad?" Katelyn demanded in her bravest voice yet. She shook with fear and anger.

"Such a clever girl," said Katelyn's mum as she slid her hand slowly across her face and became Toothsayer Tiana once more.

"I think I preferred you when you were glowing and looked like my mum!"

"A simple spell for a necessary disguise," said the fairy, moving closer to the girl. She waved her hand causing a table to slide out of the way as if pushed by an unseen hand.

"What have you done to my dad?" Katelyn shouted at the Toothsayer standing before her.

"The fool sleeps soundly and will wake feeling refreshed. That should have been you sleeping there, Tooth Bearer. Not to worry, I'll take you as you are. One way, or another, you're coming with me," said Tiana as she advanced towards Katelyn, who backed against the wall, which reached out and grabbed the young girl with clawed hands.

She screamed loudly and almost fainted.

The wallpaper, once pretty flowers, now became strong talons and sharp rows of teeth. Katelyn tried to move but she was held firm.

"Let me go!" she cried.

"Come child, or should I say Tooth Bearer, try not to squirm so. It will do you no good in the long run. Where would you go anyway?" asked Tiana in an icy voice as she moved closer to the trapped little girl. "You are, after all, amongst friends here."

Katelyn glared at the tall fairy before her. She wore robes of purple and black and upon her head was a conical hat that seemed to spiral as it reached its point. Her face was lined with age and she spoke with a commanding voice that could not be ignored. Her fairy wings were streaked with red at the tips. She did look oddly familiar, however.

"Miss me Cake Tin?" Sharpclaw snarled as he held Katelyn tightly in his grasp. She tried to wriggle free but couldn't escape his grip. His claws felt cold, like stone against her yellow hoody.

"Who are you and what do you want?" cried Katelyn as she tried to break free.

"My dear child, allow me to introduce myself. I am Toothsayer Tiana. The Toothsayer to King Pontin, and soon to be a saviour of the realm of fairies. Where others, mentioning no names my dear, have failed in their mission, I will succeed," the Toothsayer said, with bravado in her voice as if she had won already.

"What do you want with me?" shouted Katelyn.

"This is the good bit, Cake Tin. You're going to like this!" interrupted Sharpclaw.

"You will come with us to the place where the Darkness of Disbelief, as you so brilliantly coined it, manifests. There you shall remain whilst your magical teeth protect us until it has been defeated forever and I can take my rightful place as, well, as whatever I like," smiled Tiana menacingly as she looked down at the small child.

"Cat got your tongue, little girl?" Sharpclaw asked Katelyn.

"My friends will stop you!" Katelyn shouted defiantly at the Toothsayer.

"Do you mean that little fairy friend of yours? She is no match for the likes of me, for I was a tooth fairy long before I became the Toothsayer to the King. I know every trick there is in the book!" Tiana said with a smirk.

Suddenly a bright light flashed within the room, and the aromatic smell of cinnamon filled the air.

"As if by magic, here she comes now!" smiled Sharpclaw, as he sniffed.

"Take your claws off her!" shouted a small, two-inch figure that appeared out of thin air and flew straight at the gremlin. He swatted the little figure to one side, and in doing so released his grip on Katelyn. The little girl stamped down hard on his clawed foot with her shoe, causing him to hop about in pain.

"It's that fairy Tilly, curse her wings!" he shouted as he danced around the room trying to hit Tilly, who buzzed about his head like a wasp.

Katelyn ran for the corner of the room and shouted at her dad to wake up, but to no avail as he slept on.

Tiana extended her hand and a long slender bone wand fell into her palm. She pointed it at the little fairy and said, "Glaciate benumb!"

A blast of icy blue light shot from the wand, narrowly missing the fairy and hitting the wall. Immediately a patch of ice formed where the spell had hit, freezing a family photograph in place.

"Watch the ornaments!" shouted Katelyn.

Sharpclaw tried to jump upon Tilly and pin her to the ground but she flew under him and he crashed into a table.

"Stay still fairy!" shouted Tiana as another blast of icy blue light fired from her wand, striking the table and covering it in ice.

Tilly flew up and withdrew her small pin sword from her satchel. Swiftly, she flew directly at the Toothsayer; her face contorted with anger and her sword held outward.

"I will not let you take Katelyn!" she shouted as the little sword bounced off the hat of the Toothsayer.

"Please, little fairy, what do you expect to do with that pin? Put it away before you hurt yourself. Are you truly old enough to wield such sharp objects?" laughed Tiana.

"I know you by name, I don't care who you are or were. I will stop you!" snapped Tilly.

"Oh please. How dramatic, tell me what little trick are you going to perform next?"

Tilly quickly reached into her satchel and produced a bottle of glowing, magical, sand-coloured dust which she threw in Tiana's face.

"You don't know this trick. Have a good sleep!"

The magical dust settled on Tiana's face and she tried to brush away as much of it as she could. It sparkled upon her silvery face as it was slowly absorbed into the Toothsayer's skin.

"Sleep time dust. I've heard so much about you, fairy. None of it any good!" an angry Tiana spat as she swatted Tilly across the room, sending her into a wall, where she slumped to the floor.

Sharpclaw picked up the tooth fairy by the wings and held her close to his face. "Got yer now little fairy, think you're so big and tough, do yer?" he snarled at his little captive.

Tilly tried to kick out, but he held her tightly in his grasp. "Put me down!" she shouted as she tried to wriggle free.

Tiana looked around the room for Katelyn and found her crouched in the corner, hiding behind a chair.

"Ah, there you are!" said Tiana, as the first wave of

tiredness slipped over her. She fought back a yawn, caused by the sleep dust and pointed her wand at Katelyn.

Ding, Dong!

Everyone stopped and stood staring at each other, all apart from Katelyn's dad who turned over in the chair, snored, and slept on.

"That's the doorbell, someone is here!" said Katelyn standing up.

"Well, answer it. Remember, we have Tilly and your dad so don't be brave and try anything. Understood?" said Toothsayer Tiana, pointing her wand at Katelyn's dad.

Katelyn left the room to answer the door, leaving the three awkward house guests together.

"Charades anyone, whilst we wait?" asked Sharpclaw, who winced under Tiana's stern gaze.

Katelyn returned holding a well-wrapped parcel.

"It's for me, I haven't ordered anything. What can it be?" she asked the room in general.

"Well, open it then Cake Tin," said Sharpclaw.

"It's Katelyn. My name is Katelyn!" snapped the little girl as she ripped the cardboard packaging open to reveal a small wooden door with a letterbox. She read the cardboard sleeve that came with it aloud to the room.

"Fairy doors, place in your garden or house to invite the fairy folk into your home. Will delight and amaze all those aged nine to ninety-nine. Batteries not included."

"Well, that's a nice thought from someone," said Tilly, who hung suspended by her wings with her arms folded against her chest as if in a huff, in Sharpclaw's tight grasp.

Suddenly, the fairy door jumped in the little girl's hands and fell to the floor. The little wooden door flew open and out flew a tiny female fairy holding a staff.

The fairy grew in size to that of a human and flapping her wings gently; she landed on the carpet. She looked very much like Tiana, except she was slightly younger and wearing robes of deep red. Her face although stern was also friendly. Especially to Katelyn and Tilly, who immediately knew her as their good friend, Toothsayer Timoir.

She held out her staff, pointing it at Sharpclaw, and chanted, "Tempest typhoon!"

A gust of strong wind flew from the staff and threw Sharpclaw into the wall, causing him to drop Tilly. A picture fell from its hook and hit him on the head.

"Impressive, I am glad you have remembered my teaching, my dear sister," said Tiana coolly.

"Sister!" said a shocked Katelyn.

"You will leave these people alone, Tiana!" said Toothsayer Timoir.

Tilly flew over to her old friend to stand, or at least fly beside her.

"Toothsayer Timoir, they confiscated your talisman, I thought you were under house arrest?" asked a startled Tilly.

"I am, but that doesn't stop me from using a fairy door to travel here to help my friends!" smiled Toothsayer Timoir.

"I'm so glad you're here Toothsayer Timoir, I thought Tiana looked familiar when I first saw her. She could almost be your twin," Katelyn exclaimed.

"She nearly had me fooled as well at first!" said Sharpclaw, as he sat on the floor rubbing his head.

"Tiana is my older sister. I thought her lost nine years ago when she accompanied King Pontin on his last quest to dispel the Darkness of Disbelief. It seems I was very much mistaken!" explained Toothsayer Timoir as she faced her sister.

"King Pontin..., is he safe as well?" asked Timoir.

"The last quest, I thought he retired?" asked Tilly.

Tiana ignored the question, her steel grey eyes locked onto her sister Timoir.

"It is nice to see you too, my sister. Your magic has greatly improved I see," smirked Tiana.

"A neat trick with the fairy door, little sister. I had hoped to delay you as much as I could but, oh well, what will be, will be," and with that Tiana held out her wand, pointing it at Toothsayer Timoir. "Shall we dance, my dear sister?" she said coldly. "Fulmination fireball!" shouted Tiana and a fiery ball of magic shot from her wand towards Timoir.

The younger Toothsayer held up her hand and shouted, "Impel motion!"

The fireball diverted at the last moment and slammed into Sharpclaw knocking him off his feet. The singed gremlin staggered to his feet and swore so loudly that even Tilly had to cover her ears.

"Watch your aim next time, you blind, old…, sorry, carry on!" he shouted as he spotted Tiana's glare.

Timoir raised her staff and chanted, "Bola snare." A bright blue beam shot from the staff and became a magical rope that circled the older sister. It suddenly constricted around her body and held her firmly in its grasp.

"Tether undo!" snapped Tiana and the blue rope fell from her body and landed about her feet.

"Voltaic charge!" both sisters shouted in unison and bolts of lightning flew from staff and wand, hitting each other and exploding in the middle of the room, knocking everyone off their feet.

"Stop it, both of you, please, can't you just talk!" shouted Katelyn.

The room smelt of discharged electricity and sparks flickered off light fittings and other metal objects.

Tilly tried to retrieve her dropped pin sword but received an electric shock that made her hair stand up on end.

"The King, I'll ask again, Tiana. Is he safe with his family?" Timoir shouted and advanced towards her sister holding the staff pointed towards her, the orb at the end of the magical rod glowed brilliant white. The room was lit up with the spellbinding light that it produced.

"Do you care? Do you truly care, dear sister?"

Timoir looked shocked at that last statement.

"Of course I care, how could you say such things?!"

Tiana aimed the wand at her sister again.

"We all want power, Sister dear!"

CHAPTER FOURTEEN
Cottingley

"I'm not afraid to fight you Tiana, but I have no wish to battle you!" said Timoir sternly.

"Well, this will be easy then!" and Tiana circled her wand in the air and whispered, "Gelatine pulp engulf!"

A string of bright green light flew from the wand, striking Timoir. As it hit her, the light became a solid, fluorescent green string of jelly that wrapped around Timoir like a snake twisting around its prey. The string expanded quickly, covering her in the green jelly, making it hard for her to move.

Toothsayer Timoir reacted quickly by chanting, "Glaciate benumb!"

The Jelly like substance quickly froze around her body and became ice, which Timoir easily broke free from, sending shards of frozen water everywhere around the room.

"Very well done, Timoir. I taught you everything you know, just a pity I didn't teach you everything I know!" and with that Tiana reached out her hand and with her palm outstretched, she said, "Arachnid centuplicate!"

From her sleeve ran hundreds of small, red spiders that cascaded over her hand like a waterfall and fell onto the floor. As the spiders fell, they grew in size and charged like a living, writhing carpet towards Timoir, Tilly, and Katelyn.

Katelyn jumped onto a chair to get out of the way and buried her face in her hands, shivering with fear at the scene in her living room.

"Kill them, kill them with fire!" shouted Tilly, who didn't like spiders at all and flew to join Katelyn on the chair.

The spiders poured out of Tiana's sleeve and ran across the floor, there must have been thousands. They climbed the walls and curtains, and up to the ceiling where they dropped to the floor or landed on Katelyn, Tilly and Timoir.

"Get them off me!" screamed Tilly in fear.

Timoir calmly pointed her staff at the spiders and chanted, "Floret spray!"

Immediately the spiders became hundreds of small, red flowers that filled the room with a beautiful smell of a spring garden in bloom.

The flowers sparkled and disappeared.

"Must we do this all day Sister, can we not talk like civilised fairies?" she asked her older sibling.

"A civilised fairy would have searched for us!" an angry Tiana shouted back at Timoir. Her eyes locked with those of her fellow Toothsayer.

"When you didn't return, we thought you were lost to all, Tiana. We searched, but the Darkness blocked our Seeing Stones from finding you. We sent out expeditions but found nothing. How did you survive?" responded Timoir. Her voice filled with concern.

"We didn't survive. King Pontin failed to stop the advance of the Darkness of Disbelief, and it affected him, and me. He forgot who he was, his mission, and his title. Had he remained any longer within the folds of that magical embrace, he would have forgotten everyone he ever loved as well. Be left to become a forgotten wisp of his former self forever!" Toothsayer Tiana spoke angrily as she recalled the events, but her tone softened when she spoke of the King. She paused then continued.

"So I used a glamour spell to conceal his features, and the magic of the fairy rings to transport him and…, daughter far away, to someplace safe amongst the humans. I protected his memory but concealed it from himself," she said sorrowfully. "It was the hardest thing I have ever had to do," Tiana lamented as she remembered events from long ago. "I remained hidden at the heart of the Darkness, protected, in part by my magic. For years I lived there, and as my memory slowly faded I held onto the one true goal. For I had discovered a means to halt the corruption at the source once and for all."

"This is madness, what plan would be better than King Pontin's?" asked Timoir.

"A plan that would succeed. I decided not to return until I had brought light to the Darkness. Do you remember Cottingley?" asked Tiana.

Timoir winced when she heard those words and closed her eyes, as the memory was unearthed.

"Of course I remember. The events in Yorkshire are a thorn in my side that I have borne for many years. The reason for our split. It pains me so that we lost touch with each other and did not speak," said Timoir, as she lowered her staff. Tiana followed suit, and slowly lowered her wand.

"Let me refresh our memories of those events of years past," said Tiana and she started to tell the tale of Cottingley.

"We were both tooth fairies back then, newly qualified as I remember. It was the year nineteen seventeen and, as I recall, we had recently met two young human girls near the town of Cottingley. The meeting was quite by accident I might add, however as we played with them we became friends. The two girls wanted to show the world that fairies existed, but you, Timoir, said no!"

"A decision I still stand with!" exclaimed Timoir.

"You feared that if humans knew of our existence, they would trample all over our world. So you made us leave Cottingley and destroy any fairy ring that might lead to our having existed. We left the two girls alone and lost at a time when they needed us. So they re-created us, and took photographs of cut-out cardboard figures from a book," Tiana sighed as she carried on with her story.

"Of course their parents found the pictures and soon, others heard about the girl's fairies and wanted to see us. Wanted to feel the magic. Many people believed in the story of the Cottingley fairies and the two young photographers. Famous people arrived in Yorkshire hoping to see us, to believe in us, but we were long gone."

Timoir the Toothsayer's face hardened as she stared at her sister.

"I didn't know. My judgment at the time was for the best. We couldn't stay. More harm than good would have been created and you know it!" she said, but her voice faltered as if she didn't quite believe her own words.

"More harm than good? You did not see the harm that we left behind. The reporters from the papers arrived to take statements," scoffed Tiana.

"Over time, as the story came out and the cardboard fairies were revealed, the truth became known. The humans shunned us and the disbelief started to grow and spread throughout!" Tiana stared at her sister and said in an icy tone, "You see Timoir, you are the reason for the Darkness of Disbelief infecting our world. For had we stayed and shown ourselves, well, it is all ancient history now isn't it, Sister dear!"

"I can see that I have caused us much sorrow Tiana, but what afflicts you so, that you wish to cause this family so much pain?" asked Timoir.

"When I used the fairy ring to transport King Pontin and his family away, I realised that if I could transport the King away, then rightly so, I could use the fairy rings to transport the humans here to our realm as well!" Tiana replied. "Then they would have to believe in our existence. With the humans living here as well, the Darkness would evaporate into nothing!" reasoned Tiana. She sounded so sure of herself it was scary.

"You can't kidnap people against their will. Whatever the outcome may be, it isn't fair!" a shocked Timoir said to her sister, but Tiana didn't seem to be listening and carried on talking.

"I needed to protect myself whilst I herded the humans. If I stayed too long, even my magic would fail to hold back the Darkness. My followers and I would become wisps, forgotten forms forced to roam forever, bereft of any memory. Only the first teeth of a Tooth Bearer have the power to ward off the Darkness. So I needed a Tooth Bearer and all their teeth. You, Katelyn, fitted the bill," as Tiana spoke she stared at the little fair-haired girl before her as if she was a trophy.

"So you planted the seeds to grow those fairy rings where I live?" asked Katelyn.

"Not just where you live, dear girl, but all over the country. Think of it, a whole new diverse culture of humans living amongst us. With me for guidance," smiled a sleepy Toothsayer Tiana. The sleep dust, thrown by Tilly, finally started to take effect.

"You've flipped your wings," said Tilly as she fluttered beside Katelyn.

Timoir watched the Toothsayer sway and stagger, as the effects of the dust bore down on Tiana.

"Tilly, take Katelyn away from here. Go now and I shall follow in due course!" ordered Toothsayer Timoir as she levelled her staff towards Tiana and Sharpclaw.

"Eh, are we really doing this then?" asked Sharpclaw, as he got to his feet.

"Daddy, wake up. We have to go!" shouted Katelyn in her Father's ear but he slept on, lost in a dream.

"He won't be awake for a while yet. You are wasting your time, my dear," said Tiana coldly.

"Go Katelyn, I will protect your father," said Timoir sternly, but with a kindness that gave Katelyn the strength to move.

Tilly grabbed Katelyn's arm and pulled her with all the strength she could muster to the front door, and looking back over her shoulder at Sharpclaw she warned, "This isn't over!"

"Till next time, little Tills, till next time!" he replied darkly as the little fairy pulled Katelyn out of the front door and into the bright morning sunshine.

"We can't just leave Timoir and Daddy behind!" wailed Katelyn as Tilly tried to drag her down the garden path.

"Katelyn, we must. Toothsayer Timoir can look after herself. I promise you she will be fine."

Katelyn ran across the green outside of her house not knowing where to go or which direction to take, but even she realised she had to escape.

As she ran tears streamed down the cheeks of the little Tooth Bearer. What could she have done differently to help?

"Watch out!" shouted Tilly and she pointed to a fairy ring that Katelyn had nearly stumbled into.

"That was close!" they both sighed in unison.

CHAPTER FIFTEEN
East Town Park

Toothsayer Tiana and her sister faced each other in the front room of Katelyn's family home. The neighbours on either side did not understand the events that were unfolding within. To them, it was a typical Saturday morning, full of the mundane routines that govern human lives such as shopping, cleaning, homework, and hiding the bills posted through the front door to make them go away.

The fairies circled each other in the living room, each waiting for the other to make the first move.

Sharpclaw took the opportunity to have a rummage through the family belongings.

"Really, you think this is the right time to pilfer?" asked Tiana of her accomplice.

"If I'm going to get zapped I might as well have full pockets!" replied Sharpclaw.

Timoir levelled her staff in the direction of Tiana.

"So Tiana, it has come to this. A final confrontation between us. Have we fallen so low that we cannot discuss this like decent fairies?" asked Timoir, even though she knew the answer.

"Certainly not my dear Timoir. You could easily agree to my plans and join me in this endeavour, and we will all have time for nectar tea and honey scones by the end of the day. However, I don't think you'll be doing that, will you?" Tiana replied smugly as she yawned heavily and almost fell to the floor. She steadied herself on the chair.

Sharpclaw motioned for Tiana to come over.

"You know she's toying with you, biding her time till the sleep dust kicks in. I've seen it all before with Tiberius. One minute you're up, the next you're..."

Tiana fell into the chair she was holding to steady herself like a pillow being thrown onto a bed. Her bone wand fell to the floor with a clatter and she started snoring the deep sleep only a tooth fairy can deliver.

"Rotten, filthy fairy luck!" spat Sharpclaw.

All tooth fairies carried a jar of sleep dust that they

could use as a last resort if seen by a human when collecting teeth. Tilly had used it on Tiberius to put him to sleep for a few hours, which foiled his plans and led to his arrest.

"I suspected as much when I saw the yellow crystals on her face around the eyes. I recognised them as Tilly's sleep dust. She can be a very resourceful fairy when she needs to be," said Timoir with a smile, as she picked up Tiana's wand.

Sharpclaw immediately rummaged inside Tiana's pockets. As he turned them inside out he was muttering to himself.

"Where is it, where did she put it?" he growled.

"Where is what, what are you after?" asked Timoir.

"Her potion of Molten Moonlight. I need the rest of it or I'll be a garden statue once more in a few days!" he snapped as he turned her pockets inside out. "My scales are turning grey as we speak!" he said whilst rubbing his arms together.

"She only used half the bottle then. I wondered why you were helping her, it would seem that she has quite a hold over you," said Timoir.

"Well, I wouldn't be working for her otherwise, would I?" Sharpclaw snapped. "It's not here, curse you Toothsayer!" he shouted in anger as he stamped his foot on the floor.

His eyes flashed towards the younger sister.

"Sorry Timoir, but you ain't gonna take us to prison today. I've got a vested interest in her well-being it seems, for now anyway!" remarked Sharpclaw, and he grabbed the sleeping Toothsayer's arm in his clawed hand.

He turned and snarled at Timoir "It's nothing personal, but I still need that Tooth Bearer if I'm to stay as I prefer, all soft and flesh like. You ain't getting these magic teeth either. I need them more than you do, so keep away!"

Sharpclaw held up the bag of Tooth Bearer teeth and shook them in front of Timoir. He opened his reptilian mouth to reveal his crystal tooth within, the source of magical transportation for gremlins when they come of age. Licking it with his forked tongue caused the room to be suddenly filled with a bright light and a slight smell of cinnamon mixed with the rotten egg smell of sulphur from his bad breath.

As the light dimmed, Timoir saw that the gremlin and the Toothsayer had vanished.

"Well, at least I still have you," she said as she held up the bone wand that had belonged to Tiana. She picked up the wooden fairy door from the floor as well and closed it.

Without her talisman, she had no means of reaching Tilly and Katelyn as the fairy door just went from Timoir's room to wherever the door was placed, and currently, that was Katelyn's front room.

Tiana would wake up from her slumber shortly, as the dust wore off, and she would not be in a good mood. Where would she strike next?

Timoir decided the best course of action was to return to Landon, speak to the King and try to reach Tilly from there, and seeing as Katelyn's mum was now heading up the path to the front door from her shopping trip, she decided a quick exit was the best idea.

She opened the little fairy door and jumped over the threshold, the door magically adjusting her size to compensate for the small opening. As the door closed behind her with a click Katelyn's mum entered the room to find her husband still asleep and snoring in the chair.

"Well, I'm glad you have time to sit around!" she said angrily as he slowly woke up. "What a mess, what has been going on here?" exclaimed Katelyn's mum as she saw patches of ice on the wall and family pictures that lay strewn on the floor.

"I..., I have no idea!" said the Dad.

Meanwhile, Katelyn and Tilly ran and flew down the street, unsure who was following them.

"Do you think Toothsayer Timoir will stop them both?" asked Katelyn.

"If anyone can, it is our Toothsayer!" replied Tilly, who had landed in Katelyn's yellow hood.

"I'm worried about Mum and Dad, will they be alright?" asked Katelyn as she walked along beside the road, not sure where she was going to go.

"They will be fine, we need to get away though. Someplace safe where we can blend in," said Tilly who had camped down into the hood. It was very comfortable, and she felt safe.

"I had meant to meet up with Scarlett Dorsey at East Town Park. Mum and Dad take me there most Saturdays and we play on the swings. We could go there?" said Katelyn. She looked at the ground and noticed a familiar ring of growing red and white mushrooms encrusted with clear crystals.

"Great idea, I am supposed to be observing your friend, so that works for me. I'm sure Toothsayer Timoir will contact us when it is safe to do so," said Tilly, holding on to the hood as they went.

Katelyn ran along what was once an old railway track, long since removed, but now used as a cycle path that ran straight to the park. Trees lined both sides so that although they passed by many houses, it felt as if they were in a silent forest.

They soon made it to the park where they found it was quite busy with many families out and about. The sun was out, and it felt very warm, a perfect Saturday morning to be a child in a playground. Apart from the six or seven fairy rings that were growing in the park. Luckily nobody had stepped into them as yet.

Katelyn walked into East Town Park with some trepidation, for although she had been there many times before, either walking or cycling, this was the first time without her parents and she felt scared.

"Katelyn, Katelyn, over here!" shouted a female voice that Katelyn recognised as belonging to her friend Scarlett. The girl was on one swing, her red hair blowing loosely in the wind as she flew back and forth. She was being pushed by a small boy in jeans and a tank top jumper. It was Charlie, and he waved when he saw his friend and ran over.

"Katelyn, I had the strangest dream last night. You'd never guess what happened, I dreamt that you had turned into a fairy and had brought two friends to see me and there were fairy rings and I was given this strange crystal that...," he spoke quickly, filled with excitement but that trailed off when he produced the crystal and held it up.

"If it was a dream, how did I get this?" he asked, hoping the answer would reveal itself to him.

"Well, it wasn't actually a dream, Charlie," said Katelyn quietly.

"Hello Charlie, nice to see you again," said Tilly as she popped up over the top of Katelyn's head.

"A fairy, it wasn't a dream!" said Charlie, as he nearly fell over backwards in shock and bumped into Scarlett, who had followed him over.

"Watch it!" she said and pushed him forward as she approached her friend.

"Hello Katelyn, I'm glad you could make it. I'm here with Charlie's parents, as my dad is working in the shop. Did you hear about the strange things happening in the town?" Scarlett began. "Well, I heard that some strange people were up the top of the church tower, and we saw strange lights. It's all over social media!" Scarlett said excitedly. "Anyway, say 'Cheese'!"

With that Scarlett pulled out a small camera from her denim jacket and took a photograph of Katelyn and Charlie.

"Where did you get that?" asked Katelyn, rubbing her eyes where the flash had blinded her.

"Dad gave it to me so I can be a real reporter one

day!" chirped a happy Scarlett.

"Can you call people on it?" asked Charlie.

"Don't be silly, it's a camera, not a phone!" laughed Scarlett as she placed it back inside her pocket.

Tilly flew down to Katelyn's ear and hidden from view amongst her hair she whispered "ask Charlie for his crystal, we can use it and call for help like a phone!"

"Come on you two, last one on the zip line is yesterday's news!" shouted Scarlett as she ran off, a blur of red and blue denim amongst the crowd.

"Katelyn, where are your mum and dad?" asked Charlie as they followed Scarlett.

"Charlie, a lot has happened and I don't know where to start. Mum and Dad are at home, and we were visited by this powerful fairy that wants to take me away and use my teeth to hold back the Darkness of Disbelief that I told you about at school!" she lamented with a heavy sigh.

"That sounds really heavy. What are you going to do?" he asked, concerned for his friend.

"I don't know, I need to call for help. So can I borrow your crystal please?" she asked.

"Sure, take it," he said as he handed the Seeing Stone to Katelyn who rubbed the smooth sides of the crystal. She held it up to the light and thought of her family and slowly an image formed of the front room in her house, where she saw her mum and dad talking and looking for their daughter. However, there was no sign of either Toothsayer or Sharpclaw.

"Well, they seem alright and Dad's awake, but where are Tiana and Sharpclaw?" she asked Tilly, who had flown beside her friend so she could get a better view.

"Show me the location of Sharpclaw the Gremlin," said Tilly as loud as she dared to the crystal.

An image formed of a pleasant park filled with many families playing together. Children played on swings and a red-headed girl flew past on a zip wire. A man wearing a dark suit and sunglasses could be seen striding towards a little girl wearing a yellow hoodie and standing with a small boy wearing jeans, a shirt, and a tank top jumper.

Both Katelyn and Tilly stared at each other and turning as one they saw the dark-suited man in sunglasses approaching. His face had a slight glimmer about it. He smiled as he saw the little girl and the sun caught one of his teeth.

It was made of crystal.

CHAPTER SIXTEEN

That's not my mum!

"Hello, Tills!" Sharpclaw shouted across the park as he saw them.

"RUN!" they shouted as one and pulled Charlie along behind them, running through families and over picnic rugs to escape.

They dashed towards the zip wire with Tilly hanging onto the hood of Katelyn's jacket; her legs flying behind her as she held on for dear life.

The man had stopped, and he was scanning the crowds, trying to find the little girl in the yellow hoodie amongst the families and playing children.

"Scarlett, run for the trees. Come on Charlie, run faster!" shouted Katelyn as she pulled her friend.

Scarlett turned around to see her mates charging towards her, screaming at her to run and hide.

"Now you want to play. I've had to zip myself twice along this line. Come on Katelyn, have a go and I'll push," she said as she jumped off the wire and held the seat out for Katelyn.

"No time!" shouted Katelyn and grabbed Scarlett's hand, dragging her along to the forest that lay behind the play area, where they ducked behind some bushes and kept their heads down.

"Stop the presses, you two, what is going on. Are we playing hide and seek?" asked Scarlett.

They looked out through the twigs and leaves and saw the man in the dark suit walk up to a woman that had just entered.

"Hey Katelyn, isn't that your mum over there with that man. Why is he wearing that suit in this weather, doesn't he know that you don't wear stripes with shoes like those?" said Scarlett as she tried to get a better view. "Wait a minute, he's wearing sandals. What a fashion disaster!" she laughed.

"That's not my mum," said Katelyn through gritted teeth.

"Who is it then?" asked Scarlett, with a quizzical expression on her face.

The woman was also watching the crowds. She held out her arm and seemed to say something which the children couldn't quite hear as they were too far away.

"Oh, no!" said Tilly from Katelyn's hood.

The crystal that Katelyn was holding started to glow with a bright light from deep within its core. The light erupted from the stone and illuminated the bushes and the surrounding area. The man and the woman turned towards the glow and walked casually over.

"Not good, not good at all!" said Tilly as she flew up

from Katelyn's hood and drew the short pin that she used as a little sword.

"What on earth is that?" an astonished Scarlett exclaimed, pointing at Tilly as she flew out of the yellow hood.

"KATELYN, RUN!" shouted Tilly.

Katelyn got up and ran into the wooded area as fast as she could with Charlie and Scarlett in hot pursuit. She turned around and shouted at Tilly to follow.

"Tilly, come with us. I need you!" she shouted.

Tilly breathed heavily and sheathed her pin. She flew after the children, closely followed by the man in the dark suit and the woman not far behind.

"Front-page news, what is going on?" shouted Scarlett as she ploughed on through some bushes.

"Just run and don't look back Scarlett!" screamed Charlie as he followed her.

"Watch out for the fairy rings, don't step in them!" shrieked Tilly as she flew behind.

"What fairy rings?" said Scarlett and added, "I can't believe I'm talking to a fairy!"

A blue light shot past the group and hit a nearby tree, coating it in ice. Snow fell to the ground, covering the group as they ran and slid on the frozen ground.

"Katelyn, you have got to tell me what is going on. This is going to be the best news I've heard all week!" Scarlett wheezed as she produced a notebook and pen and began writing.

"Really, now is not the time to stop and write!" said Charlie as he pushed Scarlett through some brambles and down into a fast-flowing river.

"Charlie Goodman, just you wait. I'm all wet!" shouted Scarlett as she stood in the ankle-deep water.

"I will tell you all when it is safe. Just believe me when I say we cannot let those people find us!" Katelyn breathed heavily, as she slid alongside her friends.

They had reached a small bridge that spanned the river that ran through the forest alongside the old railway track route now long gone and replaced with a forest walk.

The river bubbled merrily along under the bridge, and it was here that the children and the fairy were now hiding. They held their breath when they saw the couple approaching the bridge. Neither looked happy.

"Where is she?" asked the man.

"She won't get far. I shall cast an illuminating spell again on her crystal," said the woman.

The couple walked onto the small wooden bridge that spanned the river, unaware that Katelyn and her friends were hiding underneath.

Katelyn slipped the crystal deep into her pocket and kept her hand covering it to shield the light, just in case.

"Come out, come out Cake Tin. No hard feelings. It's all water under the bridge!" shouted the man.

"If only they knew," whispered Tilly from their hiding spot under the bridge.

The man turned to the woman and threw a stick into the river, he watched it sail under the bridge and out the other side.

"Want a go?" he asked.

"Really, now?" she said.

"You must do something for fun, now and again?" he asked.

"I did, once upon a time. Then I learned that life is not all about 'fun', Mister Sharpclaw," she replied casually.

He reached into his pocket and produced some beans, which he threw onto the ground beside the water. Instantly a fairy ring of mushrooms grew.

"Get away!" whispered Scarlett. "Did you see that?" She grabbed Katelyn by the arm and shook her gently. "Those mushrooms grew in seconds. That's not natural, is it?" she asked.

"No, no..., it's not," replied Katelyn quietly.

Turning around to the woman the man asked, "How come, to open a locked door, you just say 'open', yet to create ice or wind, it's a fancy word, and a song and dance?"

"Prestige, my dear Sharpclaw. It is all about prestige. You asked about 'fun', well the prestige is my fun," the woman smiled as she spoke, her eyes scanning the forest for any signs of the children.

"Let us go. They have moved on," she said.

Under the bridge, the little group sat huddled together. The water was icy and Scarlett was getting cold feet and legs, having chosen to wear a skirt that day.

"My socks and shoes are soaked and I'm cold, and I want to play on the swings. Please tell me why I'm hiding under a bridge, standing in a river?" complained Scarlett.

"Because those two are after me!" whispered Katelyn, trying not to attract attention.

"Yes, and they are creating the magic fairy rings. I dropped my torch in one and it vanished!" said Charlie.

"You two really know how to spin a story and have a fun time!" Scarlett scolded Charlie and Katelyn.

"It's not my fault that fairies exist and want to steal Katelyn's teeth away!" said Charlie defensively.

"Who would want to steal Katelyn's teeth?" questioned Scarlett through gritted teeth.

"It's true, they want me and my baby teeth because I'm a Tooth Bearer," cried Katelyn.

"A Tooth Bearer, what's that?" asked Scarlett.

"Didn't I tell you at school?" snapped Katelyn.

"I remember you talking, but I don't remember me listening!" remarked Scarlett.

Katelyn sighed and turned her eyes upwards in despair.

"A Tooth Bearer is a person whose first teeth can save the fairy realm," replied Katelyn as she kept her gaze locked on the couple hunting for them.

"Well, they can have my baby teeth, I've got plenty!" moaned Scarlett again.

"They'd never get them out, you keep talking so much," laughed Charlie as quietly as he could.

"I'm sure you've got some spare teeth I can give them Charlie Goodman!" said an angry Scarlett.

"Come on you two, you're my friends, and friends don't fight!" pleaded Katelyn.

"Quite right. We haven't been introduced, my name is Tilly Lightfeather and I am a qualified tooth fairy, and Katelyn's friend. What she told you is the truth, and right now we are in a lot of danger!" whispered the little fairy.

"Pleased to meet you," shivered Scarlett quietly as she crouched low, hugging her knees to keep warm.

The group watched the figures of Katelyn's mum and the man in the dark suit talking together. They were the only people in the area and it was silent, save for the odd bird call.

All of a sudden the woman moved her hand across her face and transformed into Toothsayer Tiana, her fairy wings sprouting out from her back. The man transformed, growing horns and bat-like wings, to become Sharpclaw once more.

"I quite enjoyed wearing that suit. Next time I come to this realm I'm going to steal myself one," said the gremlin. "Cufflinks as well, I want some nice cufflinks," and he peered over the bridge towards the group of children hiding below, though he did not see them at first.

"Oh my, what is that thing?!" shouted a terrified Scarlett, and without thinking she jumped up and pointed at the gremlin.

Tiana and Sharpclaw dropped their gaze to see the little group huddled together under the bridge. A smug smile sat upon the faces of Tiana and her ally.

"Well, well. Didn't your parents tell you it's rude to point little girl!" snarled Sharpclaw at the terrified Scarlett as she stood, frozen by fear in the water.

"It seems that the Tooth Bearer has brought her friends along for the ride. Grab them Sharpclaw, grab them all!" said Tiana with menace.

"Hello Tills, so very nice to see you again, and so soon as well. I missed you!" grinned Sharpclaw, revealing a mouth full of sharp teeth.

"Who are your friends Tooth Bearer, why don't you introduce me?" asked Tiana as she casually walked towards the group as if at a dinner party.

"You keep back!" shouted Tilly, fluttering up so that her face was at the same height as Tiana's.

"What do you think you can do, little fairy? So small and so brave. Do you think you'd have a chance against me, a powerful mage?" asked Tiana slyly and pushed Tilly out of the way with ease as one might brush a fly away.

Scarlett Dorsey stood up and making her hands into fists stomped towards the Toothsayer. Her face was red with anger. Katelyn and Charlie jumped up behind her and tried to hold her back, but to no avail. They couldn't stop her.

"We may not have your magic, but at least we don't have to hide, and pretend to be other people. Why don't you pick on someone your own size and go away? We don't want you!" she shouted with a wave of anger in her voice that made Tiana wince.

"Who do we have here, so fiery and full of anger?" asked Tiana as she examined the red-headed girl.

Scarlett stopped and stood, staring at the Toothsayer before her. Neither she nor Tiana said anything for a minute, their eyes locked together like two magnets. Finally, the Toothsayer asked, "Do I know you from somewhere girl?"

"Yeah, you read about me in the funny papers!" and with that, Scarlett produced the small camera from her pocket and quickly took a photograph of the fairy. The flash on the camera went off and blinded Sharpclaw and Tiana momentarily with the bright light causing them to stagger backward.

"Now RUN!" shouted Scarlett.

"She's done it now, I'm turning into a statue again. They are all the same, these humans with their evil inventions. Help me!" wailed Sharpclaw as he spun around on the ground, kicking and thrashing at the air. Tiana sighed heavily as she watched everyone.

"Oh please, give me strength. The Molten Moonlight potion protects you from bright light. You are not turning into a statue, Sharpclaw. Didn't you ever wonder why you could walk in the light? Now go, get after them, you fool!" shouted Tiana at the gremlin as she watched the little group running up the river as fast as they could against the current. "Was it her..., after all this time?"

She moved forward and held out her hand, pointing a finger at the river, and chanted the words, "Glaciate benumb!"

A sharp blue light shot out of the Toothsayer's finger and struck the water, immediately freezing it. The ice quickly spread across the river towards the fleeing group and caught them up. Over they went, sliding and slipping, unable to gain a foothold on the water as it froze beneath them.

"Oh no, I can't stop myself!" shouted Charlie as he flipped up on the ice and rolled like a bowling ball into Katelyn, knocking her head over heels.

Tilly, who had been flying overhead, looked up and saw where the tumbling group would end up. Right into the middle of a fairy ring of red and white spotted mushrooms.

"Katelyn, look out!" she shouted as she dived like a plane towards her friend, hoping to save her. It was too late though for nothing could stop them.

Katelyn, Charlie, and finally, Scarlett rolled and slipped into the fairy ring, vanishing in a flash of bright light.

Tilly closed her eyes as she watched her friends disappear, and under her breath, she uttered, "In for a tooth, out for a pound then!"

She flew straight at the fairy ring and vanished

within its circle. A fading light marked the spot where she had entered.

Sharpclaw and Tiana came striding up behind the group just in time to see them fall into the circle.

"So, do you want me to follow, because I'd rather know where I was headed first?" Sharpclaw asked Tiana apprehensively.

The Toothsayer sighed and clenched her fists.

"No, we both have a train to catch at Clare station tonight. An old friend of yours will meet us there. I will deal with our troublesome foursome in good time, don't you worry!"

The pair turned around and headed back into the park. The Toothsayer casually moved her hand over her face and became Katelyn's mum once more, and Sharpclaw was transformed into the sharp-suited man in the sunglasses and sandals.

"You could have given me loafers or something better on my feet," the man said.

"Trust me, only sandals will contain those giant claws, and will you please use some foot deodorant!" the disguised mum said bluntly as she walked into the crowded park.

The forest became silent again, save for the cracking of the ice on the thawing river.

CHAPTER SEVENTEEN
The train without tracks

Considering that it was a Saturday night, the small picturesque Suffolk town of Clare was very quiet indeed. The well-tended park, popular with people having picnics, was empty. In one corner sat the remains of an old ruined castle, stripped as many castles had been over the years of nearly all its stone, sat high atop a hill overlooking the pointed rooftops of the many houses and the remains of the old railway station that sat within the grounds of the park.

Closed down many years earlier, all that remained was the station and its little café, the platform, and nearby goods shed that had been converted into a function room. The track area was now a lawn for the people of Clare to have their picnics on. No more would you be able to smell the coal smoke or hear the steam whistle blow as trains ploughed along the line, delivering goods from east to west.

At least that should have been the case and both Harry and Terry, two local lads who liked nothing more than racing their cars around the twisty streets or meeting their mates in darkened supermarket car parks to talk about sound systems and engine tune-ups, would have agreed if they hadn't driven into the park at Clare that night for a meetup, and seen a sight so astonishing that, had they had any sense, they would have spun around and raced off.

Instead, they investigated the station platform that was strangely lit up and covered in pale blue and amber smoke that poured down the sides of the platform onto the area where the railway tracks once sat.

They investigated the bright shining light that blinded them at the front of what they could only describe as a giant steam locomotive. It sat huffing and puffing with pale blue smoke pouring out of the chimney that sat on top of the engine's black boiler.

The giant wheels that propelled the engine sat on tracks that had long since been taken up so it looked as if the wheels were sitting slightly in the lawn where the railway tracks once lay.

The bright green paintwork on the body of the engine gleamed and the brass lanterns that hung from the boiler shone brightly through the steam, lighting up the nameplate which read 'The Royal Shard'.

As the two lads slowly walked alongside the steam train, they saw that coupled behind the engine was a large dark green tender painted with the words 'Great West-Tooth Railways'. A tender, as any train enthusiast will tell you, is a rail vehicle that holds coal and water for the engine to use as it travels.

However, instead of being full of coal as expected, this one was full of small brown and yellow objects that the boys couldn't quite make out.

Anyone else would have, by now, turned around and headed home as fast as they could, but for some strange reason, the two boys felt compelled to carry on, to move closer to the end of the train.

In the past, they had fare dodged and ridden the trains until the inspectors or police had caught and dealt with them, but this time neither of them felt inclined to board the carriage that sat coupled to the rear of the tender.

The final wooden carriage that scared the normally brave pair of lads, looked ordinary to start with for it was painted a deep green, with frosted glass windows framed by plush red curtains which ran down both sides of the bodywork.

However, towards the rear of the train, the wood panels gradually changed on the last carriage and gave way to rough stone as if the rock had melted into the wood. Green strangling vines of ivy grew along with the wood and rock and finally snaked and spiralled around a small stone tower that seemed to grow out of the roof of the carriage. It stretched up into the sky for about ten metres.

A narrow wooden double door at the rear of the carriage led to what appeared to be a brake van that would help the engine when it slows down. A balcony opened up about halfway down the stone tower facing towards the rear and lit by a single brass lantern that swayed in the breeze, casting long scary shadows along the old railway station.

At the very top of the tower sat a pointed roof of dark grey shale slate, topped off by an old rusty weathervane that was shaped like a tooth. To the naked eye, it looked as if the stone tower had been built onto the back of the wooden brake van. How could a train pull such a structure?

Dumbfounded, Harry and Terry walked along the platform in silence until they arrived at the small wooden door in the brake van. As they drew closer, fearful of what might live within, the door opened, and out stepped a small, thin middle-aged man wearing an oil-stained jacket over blue overalls and wearing a flat cap. He was eating a jam pasty.

"How-do, lads?" he said through a mouthful of pasty crumbs that flew everywhere, as he climbed onto the platform and withdrew a brass pocket watch from his overalls, which he duly checked against the time on the station clock.

"Ten minutes late, not a good start. My name's Beeching, that's Mister Beeching to you two mind!" he looked at each of the boys over his glasses.

"I don't want any of your cheek tonight either, so best you both get to work, and be quick about it or you'll get a flea in your ear from me!" he motioned towards the tender at the front of the train that was coupled behind the engine, with his half-eaten, cold pasty, dripping jam on the platform.

"Bad enough I can't finish my tea in peace, I've now got you two slow coaches to deal with. Well come on, the old girl will not fill herself up so grab a shovel and start shovelling those teeth into the firebox, do a good job, and get her hot enough, and you'll be able to cook a potato for your dinner in there. Well go on, what are you waiting for?"

Harry and Terry stood open-mouthed as they stared at the little man, unable to move or think.

"Right sunshine, yes I get it. I'm a sprite and I'm currently the same size as you, and yes, these things wiggling out of my head, all of my kind have them!" Mister Beeching said, as he motioned to the two small antennae that protruded from his forehead with his pasty, which promptly dripped jam onto his overalls.

"Oh, dentures and cavities," he stammered and grabbed a shovel that was nearby and angrily walked towards the engine. The two boys followed him, unable to do anything else.

"Look, it is all about magic. I don't fully understand it, but then I'm not paid to understand magic and neither are you. So just go with the flow and do as I say. Understood?" He looked from one blank-faced boy to the other and sighed before speaking.

"You two are under a short-term charm spell, so don't worry, lads. Means I must do most of the thinking until it wears off, which will be in a day or so, but nothing new there I guess," he said as he walked along the platform and stopped at the footplate of the steam engine's cab.

He pointed inside the driver's compartment and

said, "Now in there is the firebox, you shovel the old teeth into the firebox until the fire gets really, really hot. Understand?"

The tender stood coupled to the main engine and contained millions of different types of teeth, from incisors to molars. Yellow teeth, black rotten teeth, and even teeth with fillings lay strewn about on the engine floor.

Finally, Terry could speak, and he pointed at the tender and stammered, "But they're…, they're all human teeth in there?"

"Yes, what do you expect our train to run on then, fairy dust and sugar crumbs?" the sprite said in an agitated sarcastic tone. "It's not a dental diesel you know!" he quipped as he mopped his brow with a red handkerchief which he had pulled from his oily blue overalls whilst balancing his lunch on the train footplate.

"Of course, if you boys looked after your teeth more, then we wouldn't need to carry so many rotten teeth with us. You just can't get the quality anymore. Personally, I blame all the sugar in your food," he said, as he took a large bite from his pasty, scattering crumbs and jam over the two boys as he spoke.

"Now, look sharp. I want her all fired up and ready to go for when her ladyship arrives. Understood?"

he said, handing the shovel to Harry and Terry.

The two boys did as they were told and climbed inside the train to begin the shovelling whilst the sprite sat down on the footplate to finish his tea.

"Cavities and dentures, just can't get the help these days," he muttered to himself whilst wiping jam from his mouth.

CHAPTER EIGHTEEN
The train now departing...

"Excuse me, is this where I can catch a train?" said a reptilian gravelly voice.

"Depends on how fast you can run, sunshine," replied the sprite without looking up from his meal.

The voice belonged to one of two gremlins that had appeared on the platform. The tall one carried a pair of blue fluffy dice, which he swung from his clawed hand as he spoke, and the short one carried an egg with the name Nancy written on it with a pen. They stopped beside the sprite and admired the train as steam poured across the platform, creating fog and giving the station an eerie feel.

"Well, my name is Lenny, and this here is my

nephew. His name is Pichael. I was told to be here tonight by a Toothsayer I met a few...," said Lenny.

"Indeed, you were, sunshine, and you are right on time," said Mister Beeching as he stood up and flipped open a brass pocket watch.

"Right on time for tea, it seems, five to six as usual. Really should start winding this thing up!" he said as he brushed the crumbs off his clothes and checked his watch.

"I like your train Mister...?" said Pichael.

"Beeching, and that's a nice egg you got there, sunshine. Is it a packed lunch?" asked Mister Beeching.

"What, no, it's my sister Nancy!" Pichael retorted defensively as he held the egg away from the sprite in case he tried to eat it.

"Punctual, good I like that," said a voice behind the pair and they turned around to see Toothsayer Tiana walking up along the platform, with the gremlin known as Sharpclaw by her side.

"Toothsayer Timoir, I came as requested and I've been planting loads of those beans you gave me, so I..., hang on, you're not Timoir!" said Lenny as he turned towards the newcomers, his face a poster of confusion.

"Hello Lens, not seen you for a while!" said Sharpclaw, smiling as he came into view.

"Stoneclaw, you're back!" cried Lenny, his face bursting with joy as he saw his old friend. He was running up the platform to hug him before the words had left his mouth.

"Get off me, a handshake will be just fine, I ain't tactile like you!" laughed Sharpclaw as he tried to push his friend away from him.

"I'm just so pleased to see that you are flesh and scales again, boss," said a joyous Lenny as he jumped from claw to claw as if it was Christmas day.

"I'm not Stoneclaw anymore mate, I'm Sharpclaw again. Hope you've been up to no good whilst they entombed me in stone," joked Sharpclaw to his former accomplice, although Pichael, who was watching from afar, wasn't sure if he was joking or not.

"Hello, Mister Sharpclaw. I'm Pichael, do you remember me?" said the younger gremlin.

"I remember you when you were nothing but an egg. I see you've brought a gift as well!" Sharpclaw indicated the blue fluffy dice that Lenny held.

"Stole these from that car over there, the one that's called Harry. If they'd left it unlocked I wouldn't have had to break the window," said Lenny.

"I think Harry was the owner, Uncle. That was just a window sticker on the windscreen," said Pichael.

"Well, I'm the owner now!" said Lenny, proudly displaying the dice.

"I'll take those dice. Look good hanging from my driver's cab," said Mister Beeching, and he took them from Lenny and hung them in the cab.

Harry and Terry climbed out of the train, covered in enamel powder from head to toe. In true gremlin style, Lenny swiped the dice back again and hid them.

"What shall we do with these two lads?" asked Mister Beeching, leaning down from the cab and pointing at the two boys.

"Let them go, they can tell people they were working on a train run by sprites and fairies. I doubt anyone would believe a word they had to say anyway!" said Toothsayer Tiana.

She turned towards the three gremlins and said, "The fairy rings that you have been planting will draw the humans to our realm, but I need direct control as to where they arrive. I intend to plant a huge mushroom fairy ring, infused with the same crystals from my Seeing Stone like these rings here, which will act as a beacon for every human that enters a fairy ring in this realm and drop them exactly where I want them."

"Where would that be then?" asked Sharpclaw.

"Close to the centre of the Darkness of Disbelief, of course!" replied Tiana triumphantly.

The gremlins shuffled their clawed feet, and even Mister Beeching kept silent.

Sharpclaw broke the silence when he cautiously asked, "How will we be protected from the Darkness then?"

"The Tooth Bearer teeth will protect us from the Darkness of Disbelief, but I require you to protect the teeth from my sister, who will try to retrieve them. As the amount of humans increase, so will their belief in us and the Darkness will, over time, disperse like a morning mist," replied a very confident Tiana.

"Visit the Darkness, that wasn't part of the deal!" said Sharpclaw angrily.

"The deal says you do as I say, then you will get the rest of the Molten Moonlight potion. Unless you'd rather return to stone. The clock is ticking and I don't think you want it to run out?" snapped Tiana as she locked eyes with Sharpclaw.

"I see your skin colour has turned grey already," she smiled slyly as she pointed at the gremlin.

"You have me on your team for now, but never drop your guard, as I will be there!" snapped Sharpclaw as he noticed the colour of his scales.

"I'll go where Sharpclaw goes, make no mistake. We are a team," said Lenny.

"Don't worry Lenny, the Darkness won't take away anything that wasn't there already," said Sharpclaw.

"Excuse me, Toothsayer Tiana," said Pichael from behind his egg.

The Toothsayer looked down at the little gremlin as if she had noticed him for the first time.

"What happens to the humans that enter the Darkness, will they forget who they are. The Tooth Bearer teeth can't protect everyone, can they?" asked Pichael without showing any fear.

"A good question, my little gremlin, the answer to which is no. The teeth will protect us, but the humans will, in a short time, require leadership. Luckily I am here to help them in their new lives, and remember, the more humans coming through will mean the Darkness dispels faster," Tiana said smugly as if her plan had worked already.

"Mister Beeching, can we make a stop en-route at my sister's? I need to drop young Pichael off as he hasn't gained his crystal tooth yet?" asked Lenny.

Mister Beeching was about to answer when the Toothsayer interjected.

"This isn't a tour bus. Now climb aboard everyone and make yourselves at home. We have a long trip ahead of us, and I have a Tooth Bearer to find."

Mister Beeching pulled the cord that connected the steam whistle and a loud 'TOOT' was heard throughout the town of Clare. The wheels of the great engine turned on the invisible track and the train lurched and rolled forward, getting steadily faster as it thundered down the well-cut lawn until it became lost in the steam and fog.

As the smoke cleared the park was thrown into silence once again. The train had vanished as if it had never existed. All around the park though were fairy rings of red mushrooms with white spots and crystals. The only sign that something had ever been amiss was two parallel lines of burnt grass beside the disused platform, where once railway tracks had sat. An eerie silence descended upon the park, replaced only by the heavy breathing of the two boys.

Harry and Terry sat on the station platform looking at nothing, like two shop window dummies staring out of a shop window display as people walked by. Their faces were contorted into a mixture of horror and disbelief. They remained there all night long until the spell finally wore off.

"What just happened?" Harry asked Terry.

"I don't know, but I sure ain't going to tell anyone we were with the sprites and fairies!"

"Yeah, best not tell anyone that!" said Harry.

And they never did.

CHAPTER NINETEEN

Arrival...

Captain Shaw of the King's Guard leaned against the market fruit stall and prized an apple off the front, without toppling the mountain of fruit onto the floor and took a big bite. It had been a busy day.

"Put this on my tab Fred, cheers," he said to the stallholder and stood eating his purchase and musing over the day's events.

First, his commanding officer had vanished and then reappeared in some place called Kansas. He had then been tasked with arresting the most prominent Toothsayer in the city after a warrant had been placed on her wings for theft of the Tooth Bearer teeth. Then the said Toothsayer had escaped her room through a fairy door to the human realm only to return an hour later with claims that her long-lost sister had returned and was responsible for everything.

Next, there were reports of a pirate ship with a big black raven as its figurehead, flying around the desert with a metal, human-made torch strapped to its keel. It was robbing people blind by, well, blinding people with the torch.

Pirate activity in the desert areas was not uncommon as many traders had to cross those barren lands to reach the far-off cities but this was something new. Using human items in this realm was unheard of.

"Still, if there were no pirates I'd be out of a job, so they are doing me a service," said Captain Shaw to himself.

Another report claimed that some forest folk had seen a giant stray cat wearing a collar, inscribed with the name 'Pebbles' who was apparently using the trees as scratching posts and chasing the poor inhabitants about until they were all worn out.

Now he had been asked to guard the fairy ring that had grown instantly outside the Crystal Shard and had sent Captain Tyler and his men to Kansas.

So, when there was a flash of bright light and three giant children and a fairy wearing a tin hat suddenly appeared on top of him, Captain Shaw decided that his retirement couldn't come soon enough.

"Ouch, I'm sitting on something sharp!" said Charlie.

"Where are we, this isn't East Town Park? Looks like a little toy town, are we in a theme park?!" said Scarlett as she poked and prodded the nearby houses.

"This is Landon, the fairy capital city. How did we get here?" asked Katelyn as she stood up to look around and get her bearings.

"The fairy ring brought us here. Talk about random luck. We could have been thrown out anywhere!" said Tilly as she crawled out from underneath a market stall that she had crashed into.

"Help, I'm trapped under an ogre!" a muffled voice was heard shouting.

"Charlie, stand up quickly. You're sitting on someone!" said Katelyn as she grabbed Charlie's arm and tried to pull him up.

"It's a flattened fairy!" squeaked Scarlett, trying to muffle a laugh as she picked the little guard up.

"By order of King Stepney, put me down. You're all under arrest, and I'm a Pixie, not a fairy!" shouted the Captain as he struggled like a puppet on a string within her grasp.

"You are so cute, like a little doll!" cried Scarlett.

"I order you to put me down right now, I am not, nor have I ever been a doll!" shouted the Captain.

Scarlett couldn't help laughing and this did nothing to lighten the Captain's mood.

By now a large crowd had gathered at the base of the Crystal Shard. One such onlooker was Tilly's Aunt Pippa, who ran over as fast as she could.

"Tilly, I feared the worst. Thank the wings you are safe. Katelyn, wow you have grown since the last time I saw you!" said a shocked Pippa upon seeing her friend. Katelyn suddenly realised that Charlie, Scarlett, and her were not the same size as everyone else in the city. In fact, they towered over everybody else.

"Pippa, Tilly, why am I so tall, what's happened to me?" she asked.

"Nothing has happened to you Katelyn, you are your natural size and so am I," groaned a sore Tilly as she tried to stand up.

"Don't step on the market stalls, we do not allow giants in the city!" shouted Captain Shaw when

Scarlett had placed him back on the ground.

"This is so amazing, it's all so cute, I've got to take a photograph for the paper!" giggled a happy Scarlett.

"Where are my mum and dad, can I go home?" asked Charlie, looking very lost amongst the buildings even though he towered over most of them.

"Katelyn, the fairy ring in the park brought us here, but fairy rings don't shrink people. That's why they are so dangerous!" said Tilly as she stood up and accidentally knocked all the fruit over, spilling apples everywhere.

"Little sweets!" cried Scarlett as she bent down and started picking up the tiny apples like a child in a sweet shop and scoffing them.

"Hang on, you need to pay for those. All of you stand still so you damage nothing else!" shouted the Captain angrily.

"It's alright Captain, I'll take charge from here," said Pippa and she guided the children to a large open area of the market, away from stalls and people.

"Right, wait here until Toothsayer Timoir arrives. She will bring you down to size and we can sort this matter out with a visit to the King. The key thing is you are all safe," said Pippa happily.

"Hang on, I've got a Seeing Stone on me. I can use that to shrink us!" shouted Katelyn, and quick as a flash she produced the crystal from her pocket and thought about tiny things like buttons and bunnies.

"Wait, don't shrink the crystal as well!" shouted Tilly, but it was too late as Charlie, Scarlett, and Katelyn shrank to become the same size as their friends.

"Whoops!" said an embarrassed Katelyn, turning red in the face as she saw her friend's expressions. However, the Captain seemed pleased by the size change and proclaimed, "Just the size for our cells!"

"Stand down Captain By-The-Book, we are going to the palace to see the King and the Toothsayer, and you are going to escort us there!" commanded Pippa, glaring at the Captain who shrank before her withering gaze.

"Madam, I am a Captain in the King's Guard, and...," started Captain Shaw.

"Yes, and you'll do just fine for the job. Now before this crowd gets any bigger, please take us to Timoir," ordered Pippa, who stood there with both arms crossed. Nobody could refuse Pippa when she became that stubborn, not even the King's guards.

Tilly headed over to the broken fairy ring where red and white mushrooms lay scattered amongst squashed fruit of all types. She bent down and picked one up; it had the usual white spots, but also she noticed how it seemed fused with hundreds of small crystals.

"Just like the ones in Charlie's garden. What did Mariel call them, a hybrid fairy ring?" she asked herself as she examined the fungus.

"Tilly, come on. We are going to the Palace to see the King and Queen," shouted Pippa.

"Coming Aunt Pippa," said Tilly. She placed the mushroom into her satchel and ran after the group.

CHAPTER TWENTY

The tooth is out...

One hour later and the little group sat within the vast reception hall of the Crystal Palace, home to King Stepney and Queen Clement. Many paintings lined the walls, and ancient tapestries hung from the high vaulted ceiling. Katelyn sat alongside Charlie and Scarlett like three small children about to see the head teacher, looking at the paintings that hung on the wall. Most of them she remembered from her first visit to the palace, such as the one of King Pontin himself and the strange tall tower that was a Crystal Shard like the one in Landon, except this one towered above a forest.

Charlie nudged Scarlett in the ribs, and pointing at the painting of King Pontin joked, "That King looks like your dad, Scarlett."

Pippa and Tilly were whispering together in a corner of the room, beside a large bookcase whilst Captain Shaw was marching up and down, in obvious frustration at being bossed around by Pippa.

A large double door on the far side opened and in walked a group of well-dressed gnomes, pixies, and sprites followed by the Pearly King and Queen, dressed in their familiar black robes, decorated with various shiny pearls in swirling patterns. Behind the Royal pair and flanked by two guards strode Toothsayer Timoir. Katelyn breathed a sigh of relief upon seeing her old friend again.

Captain Shaw immediately bowed with respect whilst Tilly and Pippa did a little curtsey. Although Tilly ached from her crash landing she felt secretly pleased with this as her aunt had been giving her some training on how to curtsey since their last visit to the palace.

Katelyn stood up and tried a curtsey, as did Scarlett and Charlie, however he quickly switched it to a bow when he realised what he was doing.

Captain Shaw stepped forward and saluted before starting his report. "Your Highness, I have arrested these children for vagrant disregard of their size and destruction of a market stall, including fruit held within and theft of apples. Don't think I didn't see you, girl with the red hair!"

"Thank you, Captain Shaw, I don't think we will need to arrest the Tooth Bearer or her friends at the moment, and I think we can allow them a few odd apples considering what they have been through. Thank you for your diligence and dedication to duty," replied King Stepney.

He turned towards the children and welcomed them warmly to the palace. "It is good to see you again, Katelyn the Tooth Bearer. You and your friends are most welcome at this troubling time. Perhaps your arrival is as fortuitous as ever. I hope you can help us with our current situation again."

"I can try. A Toothsayer named Tiana has been impersonating my mum and trying to grow fairy rings. She wanted to kidnap me but luckily Tilly and Toothsayer Timoir saved me," said Katelyn.

"Tiana...," said King Stepney and Queen Clement in unison. They seemed shocked.

"It seems you have helped us more than you think you have. An immediate pardon for our own Toothsayer Timoir perhaps my dear?" said Queen Clement to her husband.

"Of course, right away. Never thought you had gone rogue for a minute, Timoir," said the King blushing slightly.

"Thank you, King Stepney. Now perhaps we can deal with my sister. She has quite a head start on us and I'd like to know what she is planning," said Toothsayer Timoir.

"Did Tiana say anything about King Pontin?" asked King Stepney.

"She said he was safe with his family, living with the humans under a glamour spell it would seem," said Timoir.

"Under a glamour spell, for nine years? Do we know where?" asked the Queen.

"Yes, with his mind sealed from what I am told, and no, alas we do not know his location yet," replied Timoir.

"Gnome ears and pixie toes..., under a glamour spell for nine years. My poor brother," said the King falling into his chair in shock.

"As Katelyn correctly said earlier, Tiana is intending on using the magic in mushroom rings to transport people, humans it would seem to this realm. I think she believes she can stop the Darkness of Disbelief, or control it," Timoir calmly stated.

"With mushrooms..., I am hearing everything today!" replied the King. He had sunk even lower into the chair as if to escape what he heard.

Tilly stepped forward and produced the mushroom she had taken from the market. The light reflected on the many thousands of small crystals that were embedded within the flesh.

"My friend Mariel told me that these were hybrid mushrooms because they had been fused with crystals. Isn't it normally a random area where you are thrown to when you enter a fairy ring?" she questioned.

"Normally, I would say yes. However, these aren't ordinary crystals within the fungus. They have crushed Seeing Stone Crystals within their flesh, such as the type that we use in our necklaces for transportation, and grow within the Crystal Shard itself. Tiana must be trying to control where people are deployed when they enter a ring," said Timoir as she examined the fungus.

"Is that even possible?" asked Pippa.

Toothsayer Timoir thought long and hard as she threw ideas back and forth in her head before finally concluding.

"Your Highness, it pains me to admit it, but I need to speak to someone who was once close to Tiana and King Pontin many years ago. Please arrange for Tiberius Smart to be brought here," she said.

CHAPTER TWENTY-ONE

Talks with Tiberius...

Tiberius, the flamboyant gnome who became a disgraced portrait artist of kings, and was these days serving his time in prison, had to admit that he felt rather smug, as he sat at the table with his hands casually clasped together, awaiting an audience with the famed Toothsayer Timoir and the King.

Call it fate, call it kismet, call it the luck of the gnomes, he didn't care. As clear as the ancient tapestries that hung from the ceiling or the paintings on the wall, it was his day, his destiny.

"Mister Smart, we are sorry to bring you here so late. I do hope you have everything you need and, if it would please you greatly, can we present you with the key to the city and this jewelled tiara?"

Tiberius glanced up quickly from his daydream at Toothsayer Timoir, who now sat across from him, drumming her fingers whilst she awaited a reply.

"I'm sorry, what did you say again?" he asked.

"I said that it is late, and we need you to tell us everything you know. You hold the key to Tiana!" sighed Timoir, knowing that she was in for a long night ahead.

"Tiana, yes indeed. I knew you would need my help. Please allow me to first say how happy I am that you have been reinstated in your position as Toothsayer of our city," he fawned.

"Thank you, Mister Smart, now if you don't mind...," started Timoir.

"Is the King coming to question me as well?" interrupted Tiberius, looking hopeful.

"Indeed I am!" said a voice behind Tiberius as the door opened and in walked King Stepney, followed by Captain Shaw, Tilly, and several guards who all took their seats facing the now-disgraced royal portrait artist.

"Truly, has a gnome ever been so honoured?" Tiberius said with a hint of smugness. "As radiant as ever, your Highness. You grace my presence with...," Tiberius began but stopped when he saw Timoir's face glaring at him.

"Fine, you asked me here for a reason, it is to do with your lost sister. News travels fast around this realm," he said, and sat back in his chair, resting his hands on his stomach so that he could take in the moment of seeing Timoir squirm.

Timoir regained her composure and said "We know that Tiana plans to bring the humans here using her fairy rings. She stole the Tooth..."

However, Tiberius interrupted her.

"Bearer teeth, yes, I know that. Plus she brought back the gremlin Stoneclaw as well, although I bet he's using Sharpclaw again. Don't think he really liked that rock-solid nickname I gave him!" Tiberius laughed quietly at his joke. "Tiana has put you in a bit of a pickle it seems. Without the magic teeth you can't enact the ceremony at the Crystal Shard, can you?" the gnome smirked.

"Why would she steal the teeth? If she wanted to lift the Darkness forever could she not just bring the humans here, and be done with it?" asked Timoir.

"Don't think for a minute she is doing this out of kindness. The Tiana I knew craved power and wanted to be more than just a Toothsayer to King Pontin, that's why she...," Tiberius stopped in mid-sentence and looked up at Timoir.

"Your sister was changed by the Darkness into the person she is now. Her feelings have been amplified the longer she has remained within its grasp. The Darkness whispers to you, it tricks you..., and rewards you." He paused before continuing.

"Perhaps Tiana's ideas are not her own. Perhaps they are the twisted, altered ideas of the Darkness of Disbelief. She has claimed them as her own now though, and she will see them through to the bitter end," Tiberius said coldly.

"Her plans are what exactly? We know some of her ideas, but please explain them to us so that we may understand them fully!" asked King Stepney.

"She intends to gain followers by bringing them over into the Darkness of Disbelief and converting them to her cause by making them forget their past and hearing only her voice. That's why she is using Ingress Bloom mushrooms fused with shards of Seeing Stone crystal," Tiberius commented, loving the sound of his voice.

"How did you know she was fusing the fungus with crystals?" asked Tilly.

"Well, you must have mentioned it. Is it hot in here?" answered Tiberius feeling his collar and starting to sweat as he realised his mistake.

"We didn't mention it," said Timoir sharply.

"Really, I'm sure you must have let it slip!" Tiberius shuffled uneasily in his seat as he spoke.

Tilly stood up angrily from her chair and stared across at the gnome. Her eyes burned into his soul causing Tiberius to sweat and look away.

"I believe you and Tiana have been working together from the start, Tiberius. You wanted to stop the Tooth Bearer ceremony by destroying the crystal within the Shard, claiming it was for the greater good. With our crystal gone, we wouldn't be able to dispel the Darkness of Disbelief. Which Tiana needs to convert her followers to her cause?!" Tilly exclaimed.

Toothsayer Timoir closely observed Tiberius, watching for any signs that would give him away. A twitch of an eye or a flair of the nostril. A raised eyebrow perhaps.

"Me, work with your sister. I can barely stand the fairy?!" Tiberius was going red as the questions were fired at him. His eyebrows had shot up.

"Tiberius, tell us the truth. What did she offer you?" asked Timoir. The King watched intently from the back of the room.

The gnome sighed heavily knowing that he had been found out and had said too much to stop now.

"The fame and recognition that I've always deserved, plus a small, modest statue in the market square. That's all!" Tiberius said and sank into his chair. The pontificating act he had honed had now dissolved. He decided to come clean.

"Toothsayer Tiana discovered many years ago that the Darkness of Disbelief was flooding into our world via a large Seeing Stone, held within a Crystal Shard tower that had become corrupted. I am sure you remember Cottingley, Toothsayer Timoir?"

"Those events have rested heavily on my heart for many years. My sister and I stopped speaking to one another because of it," said Timoir gravely.

"Yes, she did tell me that. It weighed heavily on her

heart for a long time as well. She got over it though. You cannot always choose your family, can you?"

"What was I saying? Ah yes, back to Cottingley!" he said.

"You appear to be enjoying this performance," said Timoir to the gnome, who glared at her.

"I will ignore that remark. When the human locals found out about the cardboard fairy figures, the Cottingley fairy rings projected the disbelief that was created, all-be-it randomly at first, straight into our realm and into the Shard which became corrupted. That in turn acted like a magnet and pulled the Darkness through and projected it over our land. The Crystal Shard in Landon acts like an opposing magnet and pushes back for a brief time, whenever you perform the ceremony," said Tiberius.

"I am well aware of what our Shard does, Tiberius," said Timoir angrily.

"Where is this corrupted Shard?" Tilly asked.

"Don't you ever look at my paintings? There is a picture of it hanging in the Palace before it became corrupted. A Tall Crystal Shard tower in a clearing, surrounded by an evergreen forest!" answered an angry Tiberius, as he stared coldly at Tilly.

"I painted that picture before it changed. It was

such a lovely forest back then. People would picnic beside the Crystal Shard."

"For a portrait artist, you are very well informed," pondered Tilly as she sized up the gnome.

"I have painted many a great person over the years, and they like to talk as I paint, and I like to listen. You should try it one day, my fine-winged friend," responded the gnome.

"So Tiana came to you, entered this city without telling anyone of her return, and offered you fame and fortune. In return, she asked you for help with stopping our Tooth Bearer. Meanwhile, she drew up plans to bring forth support from the human realm. Did King Pontin know of this betrayal?" asked Timoir.

"No, of course not. He knew the quest was dangerous, so the story of his retirement was told to all, just in case he didn't return. He took the Tooth Bearer teeth for the ceremony with him, hoping to perform the formality at the corrupted Crystal Shard. He never had a clue what Tiana had planned. He would never suspect his own..., anyway I think that the Darkness had spoken to her at this point. Nudged her in directions only it knew."

"You speak of the Darkness as if it were alive?" Timoir asked.

"I suppose I do. Maybe it is," replied the gnome. "I felt the plan she proposed was sound. Tiana believed she could control the Darkness but it was the Darkness that controlled her and still does I believe," he said as he smiled to himself.

"The trouble is that we are all unpredictable and that was why the plan failed. Who would have thought that a little human girl would be the thorn in our side?" The gnome laughed out loud.

"It was a good plan, except for the human element!" Tiberius lamented and again laughed, although half-heartedly this time, but the laughter soon trailed off as he saw the other faces in the room were not joining in with him.

"Tiana said she saved the King and his family by sending them away through a fairy ring!" said Tilly, looking shocked.

"Maybe she did and maybe she didn't. Perhaps our good King still awaits us at the Cottingley Shard. You will have to ask Tiana yourself when you next see her!" smirked Tiberius, as he finished speaking his tone turned darker as he issued a warning.

"I will say one thing about Tiana, she has spent far too long on the edges of the Darkness for it to not have affected her. The Tiana we knew back then is not the same Tiana that you have now. She will never admit it but the corruption has breached her magic and rooted itself deep within her. She has her own goals now and will let nothing get in her way. She will use you as she needs you, then cast you away as the Darkness uses her. I am proof of that, for she left me here in my cell when she could have freed me," he cried, his head held in his arms.

"Poor, poor you!" scolded Timoir sarcastically.

"After all that I did for her as well, the old Tiana would have shown more loyalty towards her followers!" he said banging his fist on the table, but then he turned towards the group and smiled as he spoke.

"Ask yourselves this, my friends. What happened to the Tooth Bearer teeth that King Pontin took with him to use in the ceremony?" asked Tiberius. "A whole mouthful sits there still!"

Just then a sprite, wearing a gold and red tunic, arrived and handed Captain Shaw a note, which he read aloud to everyone.

"Sire, this note states that as of this time, about twenty-two humans, which we know of, have arrived in our realm. The City of Light reports that three sheep, a cow, and a goat have arrived via Tiana's fairy rings. The cheese is excellent however, they say," he paused to take a breath.

"The Crescent City states that a bottle of beer

thrown into a fairy ring ended up in their water reservoir. When they recover from their headache they will submit a more in-depth report!"

The sprite quickly bowed and retired out of the room.

"Goodness, I have heard everything now. Captain Shaw, please return Tiberius to his room at once!" commanded King Stepney as he stood up angrily from his chair.

"Guess this means I will not be getting the key to the city. Oh well, such is life. I shall bid you all adieu!" said Tiberius as he left, under armed guard to his cell.

"Toothsayer Timoir, Tilly Lightfeather, you must excuse me for I have much to think upon," said King Stepney as he left the room with his guards.

"Do you think Tiana is at the Cottingley Shard?" asked Tilly as they prepared to leave.

Timoir stood up, deep in thought, and said, "No. She only has a few Tooth Bearer teeth with her, and the power they possess wouldn't protect her for long if she travelled to the heart of the Darkness. I do remember that King Pontin used the royal train to travel on his quest when he left here. The train had spells of protection cast upon it. That would also explain why Pippa recalled her saying that she had a train to catch when she saw her in the market square earlier. If she is using the train then she would have speed and protection, plus a bit of luxury as well," Timoir mused.

"Come on, let us go see the others and have a cup of hot nectar tea and a honey and chocolate chip scone whilst we decide what to do next," said Tilly trying to make Toothsayer Timoir feel better.

"Tilly, I fear that we are facing a far greater threat at our door than the Darkness of Disbelief. My sister has changed, become corrupted, and has corrupted others to her cause. If I am to face her again I fear I may not be able to stop her!"

Tilly had never heard her Toothsayer speak so gravely before and it worried her. As they left the room they saw King Stepney standing alongside his guards, he motioned them over.

"Tooth Fairy Tilly, please excuse us for I must speak with my Toothsayer alone." Tilly nodded and walked further along the corridor.

"Toothsayer Timoir, I know that this weighs heavily upon you, for she is your sister…, as she is mine, but until we know the true fate of my poor brother, please be silent from the children. It would be best if they were not told that Toothsayer Tiana was his wife and Queen of this realm."

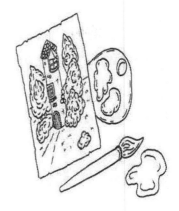

CHAPTER TWENTY-TWO

Where to go from here...

Outside in the hallway, the others had been examining the paintings that hung on the walls. Katelyn, Charlie, and Scarlett stood with Pippa starring at the picture of King Pontin.

"He was very regal and handsome, I can see what people saw in him. Wish I had met him!" said Pippa, blushing slightly.

"He does look like your dad Scarlett, apart from the ears, wings, and beard. You haven't got pointy ears under that hair, have you?" Charlie joked.

"Get off me, gnome features!" Scarlett growled as she pushed Charlie away.

"Leave her alone Charlie," said Katelyn.

"Pippa, why did King Pontin take his family with him on his quest?" asked Katelyn.

"As I recall, he couldn't bear to be apart from them, and his wife, the Queen, wouldn't let him go alone, and in turn, she did not want to leave their baby daughter. Plus they had the royal train and guards for protection, so everyone thought it would be safe. His brother, King Stepney, was to rule in his absence until his return. I guess nobody expected Tiana to pull the rug from under everyone," answered Pippa.

"I wish I had known my mum, it has always just been dad and me," said Scarlett as she stared intently at the painting of the king.

Pippa opened her mouth as if to say something but thought better of it.

Everyone went quiet and shuffled their shoes, not sure what to say, until, desperate to break the ice, Charlie said the first thing to come into his mind.

"At least I didn't get a franc for my tooth this time. I got a crystal!" he said happily.

"I have about five baby teeth left, I think," said Katelyn, joining in, and feeling her teeth.

"Fairies don't ever lose their teeth. 'One set's all you get', as my sister used to say," said Pippa as she placed her arm around Scarlett's shoulders to comfort her, as Scarlett tried to stifle a tear. She was determined not to show how she felt in front of her friends.

"I still have all my baby teeth, maybe I can be an honorary fairy?" asked Scarlett in a shaky voice.

"Of course, you'd make a great tooth fairy. We would be lucky to have you," said Pippa warmly.

Just then Tilly and Toothsayer Timoir arrived behind them.

"The King wants us to attend a meeting to discuss what we are going to do next, come on, I'll order in some tea and scones at the same time," said Tilly.

Katelyn remembered this area of the palace from her first visit when she learned of her role. She had never sat in the King's meeting room, however, as she was asked along with Pippa to view paintings of Tooth Bearer's from the past by Tiberius before he was arrested.

The room was circular, open, and dominated by a huge, round, wooden table that could easily seat twenty people. Brass lanterns on the wall hung alongside paintings and tapestries featuring famous gnomes and fairies. A brass chandelier was suspended over the top of the table. A large crystal dome in the ceiling allowed the room to be flooded with natural light.

When everyone had enjoyed their fill of nectar tea and honey scones, the meeting was brought to order by King Stepney.

"Friends, these are indeed dire times that we face, and I know not what to do. Please Toothsayer Timoir, any advice for this old king?" he asked.

"Well, my king. From what we know, Tiana has the stolen Tooth Bearer teeth in her possession and plans to grow a large hybrid mushroom fairy ring and bring forth as many humans to this realm as she can, and have them under her control. To do this she must travel as close to the Cottingley Crystal Shard as she dares. However, the fairy ring close to our Crystal Shard brought Katelyn and her friends through. So it seems our shard is acting as a kind of magnet as well. As long as the fairy ring remains intact in the market square we may pull people destined for Tiana's fairy ring to our ring instead," reasoned Timoir.

"How intact is intact?" asked Tilly slowly, not wanting to hear Timoir's answer.

"All the mushrooms must be placed or grown in a roughly circular formation, why do you ask?" asked Timoir.

"So I guess I shouldn't have picked this one up?" replied Tilly, going red as she fished the mushroom from her bag and held it up.

"No, but don't worry. We need to find out where Tiana is going and give chase in order to stop her. It is a big ask, but we do have one advantage up our sleeve in the form of the Tooth bearer herself. Katelyn has baby teeth still that would protect her from the corruption of the Darkness of Disbelief. If she was willing to chase after Tiana, we might stand a chance on getting them back and destroying her fairy ring."

"I cannot ask an eight-year-old girl to chase after a powerful Toothsayer!" said King Stepney.

"You won't need to. I will go," said Katelyn bravely.

"Me too, where Katelyn goes, I go!" said Tilly.

Pippa looked shocked and stood up.

"Tilly Lightfeather, what protection would you have against the Darkness? When you left your family home and wanted to move to the city, I took you in. When you moved to the forest, I helped you find a place to live, and when you decided to become a tooth fairy, I was behind you as well. However I cannot let my niece go off into the Darkness of Disbelief by herself and forget who she is, or worse, become something else. If you go then I go as well, and don't try and talk me out of it!"

Tilly ran over and hugged her aunt. Pippa could tell that her niece was afraid, but said nothing more.

"I'm going to be a reporter and this is the story of the century, I'm in!" said Scarlett.

"I need the toilet, but I'll go with you as long as I've got Scarlett for protection against that witch," said Charlie weakly.

"Very good, and of course I will be with you as well," said Toothsayer Timoir.

"Thank you, everyone. Captain Shaw, will you go with them?" asked King Stepney.

"To be honest Sire, I believe I should remain by your side for your protection, and help organise the roundup of any humans that end up here. In order to facilitate their quick return."

The Queen entered the room bearing food and drink. She had been listening outside.

"You are all very brave people indeed. The realm of the fairies owes you all a great debt," she said.

"How will we find out which direction Toothsayer Tiana is heading in?" asked King Stepney.

Toothsayer Timoir produced a Seeing Stone from her robes and placed it on the table for all to see.

"Show me the location of Toothsayer Tiana," Timoir said and passed her hand over the crystal.

The crystal started to fog over, then slowly cleared

to reveal the strangest train any of the children had ever seen. It appeared to be flying through the sky, speeding along rail tracks made of clouds, over a small city shaped like a half-moon, which bordered a vast desert. The scene pulled in, focusing on a stone tower that was built onto the rear of the last carriage. There, standing at the only open window, was Toothsayer Tiana. She looked up, knowing that she was being watched.

"Tut, tut, dear Sister. Didn't anyone ever tell you it was rude to spy on your family?" Tiana hissed and she clicked her fingers in the air.

Suddenly the image vanished and the Seeing Stone crystal exploded, sending shards of clear crystal across the table and making everyone jump.

"Oh, no. Whatever now?" said Katelyn, when she emerged from the floor having fallen off her chair when the exploding stones shockwave hit her.

"Katelyn, are you alright?" asked the Queen as she helped the little Tooth Bearer to her feet.

"Thank you, I am fine. Just a little scared."

"The train was passing close to a desert with a city bordering it. The Crescent City borders such a desert. That gives us a direction. We should leave as soon as possible," said Toothsayer Timoir coldly.

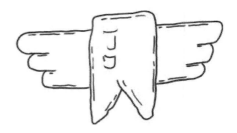

CHAPTER TWENTY-THREE
The Spirit of Landon

"So, how do we plan to give chase?" asked Katelyn.

"Would bicycles get us there quickly?" asked Charlie.

"I haven't seen any fairies on bicycles around here, have you?!" said Scarlett as the trio left the meeting room.

"I know someone who might help," said Tilly as she appeared from behind the group. "We need to go to Hedgerow airport!" she said happily, pointing towards the hills in the east.

An hour or so later the small group of friends, minus Pippa and Timoir, who were getting things ready back at the city, stood outside a collection of ramshackle buildings, water towers, and sheds. The small airport looked incredibly busy. Crowds of gnomes, fairies, sprites, and pixies, all carrying luggage and boarding passes, jostled amongst the friends as they headed to a quiet desk at the far side of the airport. A female gnome sat behind the desk. She was wearing a pale blue uniform, a little hat, and a badge with a picture of a balloon on it.

When Tilly approached she looked up and smiled. "Hello, can I help you?" she said.

"Is Stanley around, please?" Tilly asked.

The female gnome looked at her watch and tapped it a few times.

"Well, he should be in one of the flight sheds, you're welcome to go and find him. He might be feeding the Tiger Moths at the moment," she said.

"Thank you," said Tilly with a smile, and off they went, passing many other passengers heading off to the far corners of the realm. Katelyn wondered if they knew what was happening in their world at the moment and if they were as worried as she was.

Charlie looked about and wondered aloud, "I don't see any planes anywhere. How do they fly?"

"I guess the fairies and pixies flap their wings and fly themselves," said Scarlett. She took out her camera and took a few photographs.

"Wait and see," said Katelyn, and she nudged Tilly in the ribs and winked.

"This must be the place," said Tilly, stopping outside a large green barn and knocking on the large wooden door.

"Just a minute!" came the reply from within.

"I've heard that before, it's like I'm back at home again already!" said Katelyn.

Tilly laughed aloud at Katelyn's joke.

"Come on Stanley, open the door and let us in," shouted Tilly as she banged on the door again with her fists.

"Stanley, it's us. Open up!" shouted Katelyn.

"I know that voice. That sounds like the Tooth Bearer come back to visit!" came the voice from within.

Footsteps could be heard approaching and the doors opened to reveal a small male gnome with a grey beard, wearing overalls, an oil-stained leather flying jacket, and a flying cap with goggles strapped around his head.

"Well, I'll go to the dentist and back. If it isn't the Tooth Bearer herself. Katelyn, so good to see you again!" and he ran over and gave the little girl a tight hug.

Suddenly he stepped back aghast.

"Oh, sorry, I didn't mean to get oil on you. It's just so good to see you. You're not stuck here again are you?" he said quickly.

"Hello Stanley, It's good to see you as well, and no, I don't think I'm stuck here. We do need your help," she said, smiling away at her old friend.

"Hello Stanley, nice to see you again, let me introduce Scarlett Dorsey and Charlie Goodman," said Tilly.

Stanley looked at the two children that were staring at him and smiled before asking, "Are they stuck here then. I've heard stories about humans turning up just lately out of the blue?"

"No, they are not stuck here, there is a problem, however. We need to fly to the Crescent City and over the desert as quickly as possible," replied Tilly to the little gnome.

"Over the desert? That's pirate and Darkness of Disbelief territory. You'll not get a Tiger Moth to go there. They're not stupid, you know!" he said, wiping oil from his hands on a rag.

"Aren't Tiger Moths really old aeroplanes, Mister Stanley?" asked Charlie.

"Well lad, yes they are, in your world. Here they are really big insects that we fly upon. Look over there!" said Stanley, and he pointed to a nearby runway where a giant moth was seen walking along the paved launch pad. It had a special seating area strapped to its back and a pole that stretched out over its head to where a candle-lit, brass lantern hung.

A gnome in a flying suit led the insect towards a ladder of awaiting passengers. When everyone had climbed aboard and the gnome in the flying suit had settled himself at the front of the moth, the group watched as it flapped its wings faster and faster and ran down the runway before taking off into the blue sky.

"There you go. That is a Tiger Moth!" said Stanley.

"I am not climbing on that, I don't know where it's been!" said Scarlett.

"That one has been to the town of Lamp light, I think," answered Stanley.

"That would scare me so much. I've not flown anywhere yet but I'd hoped my first time would be at least in an enclosed plane," said Charlie.

"Why do you want to go into the Darkness anyway, you know what happens to people that go there?" said Stanley, with a worried expression on his face.

"I think I'd better fill you in on what has been happening since we last met," said Tilly.

Tilly explained the whole story to Stanley, who listened intently. He had always been a sombre gnome with a gruff exterior, however even he seemed shocked at the recent turn of events, and the return of Toothsayer Timoir's missing sister.

"Well, well, well. I might be able to help you out with your travel arrangements. If you can handle the excitement that is!" he said.

"I can barely handle my bladder right now," said Charlie as he thought about flying on a back of a Tiger Moth insect.

Stanley looked very proud for a moment and turned towards the large closed wooden doors.

"Let me introduce you to this old girl, she'll get you across the desert. I'm guessing you'll be needing a pilot and I know none better than I. My wife Alice always tells me I need another adventure, and this sounds like a good one. Be like old times again, right Tilly?" said Stanley.

Stanley grasped the handles tightly and forced open the large wooden double doors.

"Well, what do you think?" he said.

"What is it?" asked Tilly, squinting into the darkness. Her eyes slowly becoming accustomed to the darkness within the shed.

"What, can't you see? It's the future of passenger transportation. It will put my airport on the map for all generations to come!" he proclaimed.

The group stared at the strange, flying boat within which revealed what could best be described as a huge, flying, flat-bottomed boat with a brass and wooden keel, patched here and there with metal plates.

A steam-powered motor connected rotating paddles on either side of the hull which propelled it forward, and the whole thing was lifted upwards by a very well-patched balloon with two, large support balloons attached to both sides at the rear, which helped to keep the craft not only stable when in the air, but also stopped it from pointing down when flying.

From what Katelyn could tell, as she peered into the shed and tried to adjust her eyes to the gloom, was that two smaller propellers sprouted from the rear of the craft and she guessed that these helped to push it along as well.

There appeared to be room for several passengers within the hull and the craft seemed to be piloted from a central cabin area, where a large wooden and brass wheel could be seen, surrounded by various dials, cogs, and levers.

It all looked flight-worthy if you ignored the patched hull and escaping steam jets that blew out from the many holes that littered the keel. A wooden frame on wheels surrounded the craft to enable Stanley to work on it.

"This might just work!" Katelyn whispered to Tilly.

However, she had her fingers crossed behind her back when she said it.

Charlie glanced at Scarlett, and without saying a word, both knew what each other was thinking. He secretly hoped his parents had taken out a good life insurance policy on him. They might be making a claim soon!

"Come on, help me move the cradle and we will wheel this beauty out into the light!" Stanley motioned for help with the wooden support structure that surrounded the craft.

Slowly they pushed the ship out whilst Stanley started to inflate the balloons that would keep the craft stable and, with luck, get it to fly.

Once the support cradle was removed everyone could see the ship in all its glory for the first time.

CHAPTER TWENTY-FOUR
The maiden flight

"Well, what do you think?" said Stanley.

"I..., am lost for words, Stanley!" said Tilly.

"Excited, I bet!" he said.

"That word will do, I guess," Tilly said as she examined the machine.

"This is the 'Spirit of Landon', I built her a few months ago with the help of my family. We plan to fly her and take on the long-distance market. I can even provide in-flight meals. I bet that will impress Miss Pippa!" said a proud Stanley.

"Oh, she will be impressed, I'm sure," lied Tilly.

"You don't get that sitting on the back of a Tiger

Moth, proper food with real cutlery," he said with obvious pride.

"Spirit of Landon, what do you think to the name, Katelyn?" asked a proud Stanley as he pointed to the brass name plate that was bolted to the hull.

"I think it sounds great!" said Katelyn.

"Is it a boat or a balloon?" asked Charlie as he poked the hull with his finger. A small piece of wood fell off, which he quickly kicked under the craft so it couldn't be seen.

"It's both really. She can float in the water like a sea sprite, but when she is in the air she glides like a fairy with new wings on a summer's day. No better feeling than the wind in your beard!" Stanley beamed.

"So, it's a dirigible then, like a blimp?" asked Charlie, obviously wanting to impress everyone with his knowledge of early flight.

"A dribble..., diridribble..., diri..., yeah one of those!" said Stanley, although he sounded unsure.

"Dirigibles and blimps are powered, steerable balloons. Companies advertised on them!" said Charlie, feeling very full of himself.

"You're just making this up Charlie!" said Scarlett.

"No, I'm not, it's all true. My dad told me!" scowled

Charlie.

"Advertise on them?" mused Stanley, whilst gazing up at his balloon. He stroked his beard in thought, lost in a world of money and fame.

"Earth to Stanley?" said Tilly, nudging her friend from his dream.

"Erm..., yes?" he asked.

"The reason why we are here?" she said with a frown, her arms folded across her chest.

"Yes..., you need 'Stanley the aeronaut' and his diridribble..., diridribblegibleblimp. You need the 'Spirit of Landon!" he proclaimed. "First though she needs a maiden flight, and this would be a great test. Plus, when we get back everyone will want a ride in her after the adventure she's had. Then there is the advertising!" he proclaimed in an excited tone whilst rubbing his hands together like a small child in a toy shop, armed with their birthday money.

"Maiden flight, like in a first, never done it before flight?" said a wide-eyed Charlie.

"Stanley, what we are asking of you is very dangerous, are you sure?" said a concerned Tilly.

"Tilly, think nothing of it. I always said 'if you ever need my help' I would give it, and you need it. So count me in as well!" said Stanley.

"Couldn't a..., I mean, are you sure a Tiger Moth couldn't fly us into the...?" asked Tilly.

"Tiger Moth, no, never going to happen. They have too much sense for that. This on the other hand will get us there in no time at all," said Stanley.

Before Tilly could reply Stanley had turned and run back into the barn. He climbed up a rope that was hanging down the hull, slipping a few times, in his eagerness to show off his creation.

Scarlett and Charlie just looked at each other. Both of them knew what the other was thinking.

He reappeared on the deck, and all that could be seen of the gnome was his flying cap darting across the top as he entered the cabin area and started turning brass knobs and hitting dials.

Steam started to rise from a central chimney as the huge paddles started to rotate on the craft, and slowly 'The Spirit of Landon' hovered like an old maiden climbing out of a chair for a dance she once knew.

The craft chugged slowly forward away from the huge barn into the bright sunshine. Sunlight caught the brass fixtures and fittings and they gleamed like new as if they had been fitted that day, which to be fair they probably had.

It was as if the craft knew that this was an adventure like no other, as it lurched forward and upward, eager to take to the sky. The balloon expanding to fill the expanse of open-air with a patchwork of sewn colour. Truly this was a sight to behold.

It was obvious though that Stanley saw a slightly different machine than the small group of friends did, however, no one wanted to tell him that. The craft creaked and groaned as it crept out and holes could be seen in the hull, some already freshly patched and others still open. This was still an ongoing restoration project.

"Are we really going to fly on that? It looks like it's about to fall to bits," whispered Scarlett to Katelyn.

"Hush Scarlett, I'm sure Stanley knows what he is doing. We will be fine, won't we Tilly?" said Katelyn, turning quietly to her fairy friend.

"Sure, of course. I'm betting it comes with parachutes!" said Tilly, a little unsure of herself as she watched the vessel glide out of the barn.

"If anyone wants me, I'll be hiding in a cupboard," said Charlie as he stared open-mouthed.

A metal plate fell off the hull and landed at the boy's feet. Stanley grabbed a rope and leapt off the deck in one move, landing beside Charlie. He quickly picked it up and inspected it, before throwing it upwards onto the deck above.

"Just teething troubles lad, every maiden voyage has them. I'll just go and fix this before we get going. Reach for the sky lad, reach for the sky!"

"Is he alright?" Katelyn asked Tilly.

"I heard a lot of budget moth flights had come in and poached his normal flight routes. I guess Stanley needs this to be a huge success!" said Tilly.

"It will all be fixed, ship-shape, and ready for action, don't you worry. Now climb on board and make yourselves at home," Stanley shouted as he climbed back up the rope and lowered a little rope ladder for everyone else.

Katelyn took a deep breath, and climbed up the ladder, followed by Scarlett and a scared Charlie.

"Grab that anchor, before it stops our adventure before it has begun!" Stanley shouted down to Tilly.

The little fairy looked about and found a tarnished, golden pocket watch chain, hanging down one side of the vessel. The chain had an old watch hand welded onto the end that Stanley was using to tether the craft when it was idle.

She pulled it out of the ground and flew with it to

the deck above where she found her friends waiting.

"Are you sure Alice will be alright with this?" Tilly asked the little gnome.

"Of course Tilly, I'll send a message asking her to look after things until I get back. A friend in need is a friend indeed," he replied and pulled on a rope in the cabin which blew a brass steam whistle.

'Toot, toot.'

The Spirit of Landon took to the skies and climbed upwards, heading for the capital city. It flew over fields and small villages and as it did, fairies, gnomes, and anyone else who happened to be watching stopped what they were doing and waved. Scarlett and Katelyn waved back and watched the world pass beneath them. Charlie remained hidden below.

The world below looked very peaceful from the clouds as they flew, but from this height in the distance, at the edge of the world where the sun would later set, could be seen the Darkness of Disbelief mocking the heavenly glow.

Like a menacing, dark storm cloud of deep purple, it hung heavily on the horizon. Engulfing the land in its grasp, and causing all who saw it to feel dread.

Very soon the now-familiar sight of the City of Landon came into view. There was St. Stephen's Tower, home of William the Clock Watcher, whose job now involved winding up all the clocks in the city before they stopped.

There was Aunt Pippa's Mushroom Inn hotel, located beside the river, and there was the Crystal Shard, the striking tower that had been the focal point of Katelyn's adventures recently.

As they approached the Crystal Palace, Stanley pulled upon a lever, and slowly the craft began to descend into the courtyard. There Toothsayer Timoir, Aunt Pippa, Aunt Pippa's luggage, King Stepney, and Queen Clement, as well as a crowd of excited onlookers, all awaited them.

"How exciting, I wish we could fly with them!" said the Queen to King Stepney, who pretended to ignore his wife.

"People of the realm, the Tooth Bearer will save us once again!" proclaimed the King, and a great cheer erupted from the excited crowd.

"Clear the way, I'm landing!" shouted Stanley, and he threw the pocket watch hand overboard.

A plank fell from the keel and landed at Pippa's feet, which she picked up.

"Teething problems, nothing more, every first flight has them!" shouted Stanley as he guided the craft to the courtyard below.

"Well this is going to be an experience," said Timoir to Pippa as they prepared to board.

"I do hope this machine has hot and cold running water!" said Aunt Pippa, as Stanley helped her on board, along with her fifty or so suitcases.

"How many bags do you need?" he muttered as he hauled the luggage on board.

"My hearing is in tip-top condition, thank you very much," Pippa retorted as she headed to her cabin.

"I just hope it doesn't fall to pieces. Stanley, just how safe is your steamer?" asked the Toothsayer.

"My steamer will not let us down!" shouted the grumpy gnome.

"That's what I'm afraid of!" said Toothsayer Timoir, as she tapped the hull with her staff, before climbing up the ladder to join the others.

"Goodbye everyone, wish me luck. I won't let you down!" shouted Katelyn to the crowd of cheering people.

With the anchor back on board again, the Spirit of Landon glided upwards into the sky and turned towards their first destination, the port city on the edge of the desert known as the Crescent City, and the last place that Tiana had been seen.

CHAPTER TWENTY-FIVE
Eartha

The royal train surged through the sky at speeds that no ordinary locomotive could hope to match. As it flew, clouds formed beneath the wheels and became soft, white railway tracks that dispersed as soon as they had passed along them. Toothsayer Tiana sat in the dining carriage, slowly sipping nectar tea and eating a multi-coloured almond slice from a Battenberg cake that sat on a plate.

The table had been laid out for afternoon tea, a tradition that Tiana kept up every day, having first enjoyed many years ago when she used to meet up with the two local girls at the village of Cottingley in Yorkshire.

"Mister Beeching, I trust we are making good

time?" she asked the sprite, as he walked past towards the engine. He stopped and looked at his pocket watch.

"Indeed we are, we shall be entering the Darkness of Disbelief within the hour. All spells of protection are in place," he said.

Tiana rummaged in her robe pockets and produced a small statue made of rough clay.

"Take this statue and place it upon my desk, I will require it to control the distribution of the Ingress Bloom seeds."

"As you wish Toothsayer Tiana, may I just say that Eartha gives me the creeps? It's not natural," said Mister Beeching, as he stared at the rough statue. It resembled a very badly shaped human, moulded out of brown clay and soil.

"You may say that, but Eartha serves its purpose well and asks no questions. Do I make myself clear, Mister Beeching?" replied Tiana casually.

"As clear as crystal, Toothsayer!" answered Mister Beeching, humbly bowing as he departed.

"Good, then please send Eartha in with some more cake, and have the Ingress Bloom seeds ready to be sown the moment we land. We must create a fairy ring big enough to pull hundreds of humans through at once," Tiana ordered as he left, then she turned her attention to the trio in front of her.

She dabbed the sides of her mouth carefully before pushing the empty plate away, obviously enjoying the game of keeping her three accomplices waiting. In front of her sat Sharpclaw, Lenny, and Pichael, who had sat watching the cake being eaten, and wishing that she had offered them a slice.

"You wanted to see me then, Sharpclaw?" she said, as she placed a napkin on her plate.

"Right, look, I've done all you asked. I even dragged your sorry bones away when Timoir and Tilly bested you at that girl's house. Today, I awoke to find this!" he said, holding up his claw to reveal that it had once again, turned to stone.

Tiana calmly produced the bottle of Molten Moonlight and handed it to the gremlin, who snatched it with his good claw and rubbed the lotion on his granite fist. Instantly the rock skin subsided and became green reptilian skin once again. The bottle was still warm to the touch and glowed red. It was about half full.

She held her hand out, without saying a word.

"Why don't you just let me use it up and be done with this curse!" he snapped at her, as he slammed the bottle on the table in front of Tiana.

"Well, for one, I don't trust you. As long as you do as I ask, the potion will remain warm enough to restore you," she said.

"I don't trust you either. I wouldn't trust you if you were the last fairy in all the realm, and I was spitting out a loose tooth!" he growled back.

"Well then, that's something we both have in common. Neither of us trusts the other. I truly think we have moved forward with our distrust of each other today. I'm going to celebrate this key moment in our relationship by noting it in my diary!" Tiana said, dripping with sarcasm.

"Why don't you just give Mister Sharpclaw the potion? It's not fair," said Pichael.

"Life isn't fair little gremlin," she said bluntly.

"So, pleasant weather we've been having lately," said Lenny, trying to lighten the mood and failing.

Pichael started drawing on his egg, trying hard to make himself smaller.

Sharpclaw shot him an unpleasant glance, then looked up as he heard a dull, thudding noise that got louder and louder as if someone was throwing wet, sloppy mud at the floor at regular intervals.

"So where is this train headed then?" he asked Tiana, glancing behind her to where the noises were coming from.

"Just inside the Darkness of Disbelief. Not too far in or my magic won't protect us, but enough to set up my fairy ring and curse the humans that I pull through," she said triumphantly.

The wet sloppy sounds got louder and were now accompanied by a metal rolling sound as well.

"STONE THE GNOMES!" Sharpclaw shouted at the top of his voice and pointed behind Tiana.

Lenny quickly covered Pichael's ears, even he was shocked at the language being used.

Pichael grabbed his opportunity, and lunged forward during the commotion, stealing himself a slice of cake to eat.

"What in the name of a pox-ridden pixie is that?" blurted Sharpclaw.

Lumbering along from behind Tiana, and pushing a little maid's trolley laden with fancy cakes approached a very unusual sight indeed. It was roughly human-shaped, covered in vines and moss with the occasional flower poking out from its body. It didn't speak to anyone or even acknowledge the group sat at the table, but it did stop beside them. On what passed for a head, was a dainty, little maid's hat.

"This is Eartha, my mud golem and obedient servant," said Tiana.

"Looks like a walking vegetable patch, and smells like one as well!" said Sharpclaw.

"Hey, look, it's got some carrots in its chest!" said Lenny, eagerly pulling out some of the vegetables.

"Do you mind? Put them back now!" said Tiana crossly as she stared at Lenny. "Eartha is a golem. A mindless puppet of my creation, made from the soil in my garden. It obeys without question as long as I have its statue. Eartha would follow me to the ends of the earth and back if I asked. It also makes a mean Battenberg cake!" explained Tiana happily.

Pichael carefully placed the stolen cake back onto the table.

The mud golem proceeded to collect the plates and refill the teapot, before moving on down the carriage towards the kitchen. When it had walked off Tiana carried on talking.

"So, to matters at hand. I have discovered that the Tooth Bearer has decided to chase after us, aided by her troublesome friends and my sister."

"How did you learn that bit of information then?" Sharpclaw asked Tiana.

"I consult the Seeing Stones often. They show me all sorts of useful things. So, Lenny, stop poking around the bookshelves until you can read. Clear!"

"I like looking at the pictures!" Lenny said defensively.

"It seems that my sister has acquired the help of an aeronautical gnome, and they are currently flying after us in his flying machine. I can only guess that they intend to stop the creation of my giant fairy ring. I need to make sure that they don't succeed!" she said sharply. "The Tooth Bearer is with them as well," she said and glanced out of the window at the passing clouds as if she expected Katelyn to appear.

"She's a brave one, that human girl!" said Sharpclaw.

"She's beat us a few times, hasn't she Sharpcl..., Ouch!" blurted Lenny, now rubbing the spot on his head where Sharpclaw had hit him.

"So, I guess you need us to do something about them. Right?" asked Sharpclaw.

"Spot on, I see that we are on the same page these days, Sharpclaw. I am so happy, how very, very exciting," sneered Tiana.

She pulled an object out of her bag.

"This is a fairy door. My sister used one earlier, and to be honest, I didn't think you could teach an old fairy new tricks. However, I was proven wrong!" she laughed to herself.

"I know how these work, I was there!" said Sharpclaw sharply.

"Indeed. Now, I know they will need to stop at the Crescent City for supplies and such like, before they cross the desert, just like we did," Tiana responded. "I planted a fairy door there before we left that city, and I want you to return there through this door, grab the Tooth Bearer when she arrives, and jump back through with her as your prisoner. Is that clear?" she asked the gremlins.

"As clear as the mud on your golem," replied Sharpclaw darkly.

"Excellent. As for her friends, you can be as creative as you want in your efforts to stop them. Now off you go!" Tiana commanded the trio.

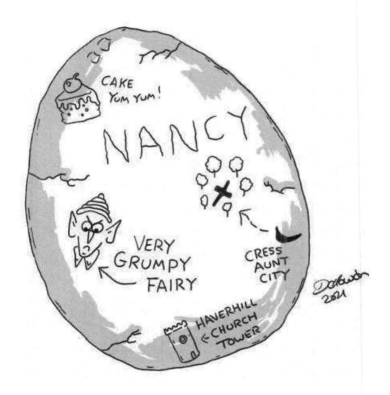

CHAPTER TWENTY-SIX

Shore leave

Meanwhile back on the Spirit of Landon, Stanley had unrolled a large map in one of the cabins and was trying to plot the quickest route to the Crescent City.

"We can't go through the Darkness of Disbelief that's pushed into these places, we'd never come out the other end. So, that leaves crossing the Desert of Lost Wisdom. We need to fly along the Enamel Coast to reach the city easily and then we can stop for supplies and take on water," he calculated.

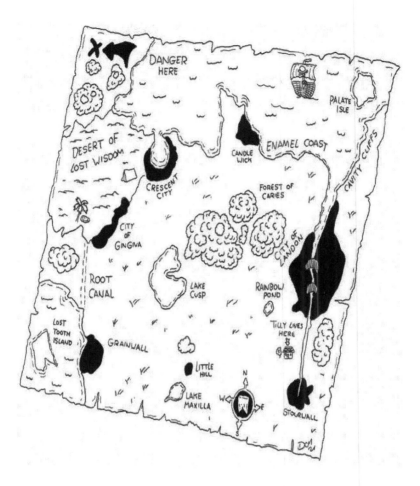

"How far has the Darkness pushed into the land recently?" asked Katelyn.

Tilly had the answer.

"Too far, ever since the time spells were broken that used to hold the Darkness back. We have seen it cover several hundred miles in just a few months, and the towns in the area have had to be evacuated, and the people relocated. They are ghost towns now."

Pippa had a puzzled look on her face as she stared at the map laid out before her.

"The Darkness doesn't push into the desert at the same speed as elsewhere, is that because it's just empty of life?" asked Pippa, as she stared at the map.

"Good question, I would hazard a guess that the Darkness works on a collective belief, or in this case, a collective non-belief, and so cannot make any ground in an empty desert devoid of life," reasoned Timoir as she entered the cabin.

"Stanley, if you are here, who is flying this vessel?" she asked sharply looking up from the map.

"Well, that little boy seems to have taken to piloting like a fairy to a tooth. He's got that girl with red hair with him, so he'll be alright!" said Stanley.

"Oh well, that's good to know then. Only two minutes' flying experience and Charlie's been given the wheel!" said Timoir with a concerned, sarcastic voice that everyone noticed.

Stanley frowned and ignored her.

"It is getting late. We had better land and set up

camp for the night and get a good night's sleep," said Stanley, as he headed upwards to where Charlie and Scarlett were.

"Be nice please Timoir. Stanley is helping us," said Katelyn.

"I'm sorry, I will apologise to him. I am just so worried about my sister and her plans. I've just heard that twenty more humans, two cats, and four dogs have appeared in our realm. We are having trouble containing and sending back those humans that are already arriving," Timoir said sadly.

Katelyn held her friend's hand as she listened.

"What will it be like when Tiana plants her fairy ring and pulls hundreds of humans through into one place?" Timoir looked suddenly very old, alone, and unsure of what to do next.

"I sometimes wonder if I should have just agreed to her plans at Cottingley, all those years ago," she sighed.

"If ifs and buts were candy and nuts, the tooth fairy would never retire!" said Aunt Pippa.

That broke the mood and they all laughed. Moments later they felt the craft start to descend as the wooden hull creaked and groaned.

"I had better get the tea on, Tilly can you help me make some cakes and grab the bottle of Honeydew?" said Aunt Pippa as she tied an apron around her waist.

"Of course, be like old times," said Tilly happily.

Katelyn smiled at the old Toothsayer and walked over to her. She took Timoir's hand in hers again and said, "Let's go look at the stars together!"

"I would like that Katelyn," Timoir responded and patted Katelyn's hand warmly.

They landed within a small clearing in a forest. The craft was quickly anchored in place and Pippa and Tilly set about cooking tea.

They all enjoyed a lovely picnic under the stars. They ate human cakes, which were the same as fairy cakes, but without the wings. Warm honeydew milk was served and hot nettle soup, with fresh, gnome baked nutty bread was eaten. It wasn't long before the little group was tucked up in their bunks, fast asleep.

The next morning Charlie and Scarlett were up early. It was a warm spring day and the first dew of the day had settled on the forest, coating it in dainty beads of watered pearls. The jewellery of the morning, as it was known.

"Shall we go and explore the trees, they look so

pretty?" said Scarlett, eager to stretch her legs.

"Shouldn't we wake Katelyn and the others first?" Charlie asked.

"I'll leave her a note, come on. The last one over to that tree is a sleepy gnome!" she shouted and climbed down the rope ladder that hung over the side of the hull and started running.

"Wait!" said Charlie as he tried to catch her up.

The forest did indeed look lovely, but as any fairy knows, danger can be hidden behind every tooth.

They ran and ran, cheering as they went, happy to be young and free to do what they pleased.

All of a sudden, Charlie slipped over having skidded on something on the ground. As he tumbled over he tried to prevent his fall with his hands but he landed in something soft, slimy, and green.

Trying to stand he slipped over again. The green slime stuck to his hands and feet and he couldn't shake it off. It smelt like old, dirty pond water and he wrinkled his nose as the scent hit him in the face.

"Oh, gross. That's just yuk!" he said to the forest.

If it was listening it didn't answer him. He turned around but struggled. He felt like he was standing in glue or cold porridge. As he lifted his leg the slime came with it and he fell over again.

"Ouch, yuk!" he said as he struggled to his feet. His hands were covered in the green slime. "Scarlett, come here and help me!" he shouted to his friend, who stopped running and walked back.

"What have you done?" she asked. When she saw him she burst out laughing, as he looked like he had plunged his hands into a lime green jelly, and his feet were encased in the slime as well. He did look a sorry sight.

"Don't you laugh, you're standing in it as well!" he said.

"Oh, gross. Get it off me!" she cried and tried to lift her feet but they were stuck as well and her shoe came off. "I've been sneezed upon!" she shouted angrily.

"Scarlett hush!" said Charlie.

"Hush yourself, slime boy!"

"No, be quiet!" said a scared Charlie.

Scarlett saw his face and closed her mouth.

"What on earth is that over there?" asked Charlie as he tried to clean his glasses.

Scarlett turned her head and squinted at the strange sight that slowly approached them. Both Charlie and Scarlett stared and stared, unable to tear their gaze away.

They were rooted to the spot as if they were part of the forest itself.

Unable to move.

Was that a shadow that they saw move in between the trees as well, watching them with hungry eyes?

It mattered little as the children's faces had become glazed over, transfixed by the sight that slowly slid towards them leaving a trail of green slime as thick as yesterday's cold porridge.

To the casual observer, the creature looked like a giant snail, roughly about the size of a small horse, with a colour spinning shell upon its back. The colours danced from the spiralled centre of the shell as if alive and radiated outwards like a cascading rainbow of light patterns.

Caught in the mixing of this vibrant palate, a person, be they of this realm or not, could do nothing but stand and stare, unable to move until the creature had passed. Worse still if you accidentally stepped in its slime trail there was a good chance you would become stuck for hours.

This was this gentle giant's best defence.

The fear that every victim had was not the snail itself but from what followed these slow-moving beasts, waiting to feast upon any weary soul that had accidentally happened upon this creature and become rooted to the spot, an easy meal indeed.

The snail might have had a protective shell to hide when in trouble, but Charlie and Scarlett did not.

Things were not looking good for the two children for they could not call out for help or move.

As the snail passed by a soft clicking sound could be heard from the forest behind it.

The clicking sound got louder and louder then quieter, almost as if something was circling the children.

Watching them.

Waiting to strike.

Waiting to eat.

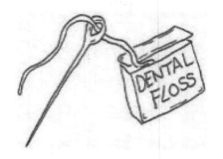

CHAPTER TWENTY-SEVEN
Never mess with a tooth fairy!

Back at the camp, Aunt Pippa was busy preparing breakfast of eggs and toast. Timoir and Stanley were talking quietly together whilst Tilly and Katelyn, who had both just got up, were sat together on the deck listening to the dawn chorus playing out across the treetops as the creatures that lived there woke up.

"This looks like the forest you live in, Tilly!" Katelyn asked her friend.

"I do miss my home, the mornings are lovely when you hear the birds singing first thing," Tilly said.

Katelyn looked over to where Stanley and Timoir were talking quietly.

"I think Timoir is making her apology. I feel sorry for her, but I do understand her thinking that it would be dangerous to have full-sized humans marching about the land. She needs people to believe, just not visit all at once," sighed Katelyn.

"Talking about people visiting, where are Charlie and Scarlett?" asked Tilly, her eyes scanning the deck and campsite for the two children.

"I thought they were still asleep. Hang on, I have a note in my pocket!" Katelyn said as she produced the little letter she had found. "It says, 'You were still asleep so we have gone to explore, be back before breakfast'. Where have they gone?"

"They should know better than to explore the forest without us. Come on, we'd better go and find them," said Tilly grabbing her helmet and bag.

"Don't you two be long, I'll let the others know and I'll contact you if Charlie and Scarlett turn up!" shouted Pippa after the two friends, who were already running across the grass into the forest.

As soon as they entered the forest the light changed and it became darker. The trees took on strange shapes that loomed over the pair and the air became cooler.

The dawn chorus seemed to mock the pair as they searched for the two lost children. Where were they?

"CHARLIE, SCARLETT, where are you?!" shouted Katelyn and Tilly together.

"Why aren't they answering us?" asked Katelyn.

"Look over there, I think I see them!" said Tilly, pointing into an open clearing.

Katelyn ran through the trees, jumping over logs and stumps until she entered the clearing and stopped suddenly.

"Don't look at the shell, it's a Mirage Snail and it'll hypnotise you!" shouted Tilly, grabbing her friend's shoulder and spinning her around, away from the creature.

This Mirage Snail was a lot bigger than a normal

Mirage snail and must have been very old. The top of the cracked and worn shell easily reached Tilly's shoulders. As it slowly crossed the clearing you could hear a sucking sound as its body slid along the forest floor leaving a trail of sticky slime.

It made its way slowly across the clearing leaving a trail of green slime in its wake, whilst both Charlie and Scarlett stood staring, glued to the spot, transfixed by the colourful shell.

"Mirage Snails are harmless, but watch them for too long and you'll be there for hours, unable to move, rooted to the ground!" said Tilly to Katelyn. "Some fairies hitch them to carts, so long as you're not in a hurry and don't stare directly at the shell. They can pull cartloads of trade. Now, don't move and don't look at the shell!" she commanded Katelyn in a strong, forceful voice.

"If they are harmless, what's the problem?" asked Katelyn, starting to shiver at the change in Tilly.

"They are harmless, but other creatures follow them and use their hypnosis to pounce on their stuck prey!" said Tilly, slowly drawing her pin sword and watching the tree line. "Thimbles and needles, I'm not strong enough to fly you all out of here!" said a watchful Tilly.

She heard a soft clicking sound.

She froze and raised her pin sword.

The clicking sound began again but much louder.

"Tilly, do you hear what I hear?" asked Katelyn.

The pair stood staring into the forest, their breaths were the only noise to be heard, save for the strange clicking sound that interrupted the silence.

By now the Mirage Snail had moved off into the forest and was nowhere to be seen. They were on their own. Fear crept into their bones.

"Charlie, Scarlett. Are you alright over there?"

Katelyn tried to sound brave but her voice gave out. It mattered little as neither of the other children responded to her plea.

The soft clicking sound carried on, then stopped. Tilly stared at the shadows cast by the trees and thought she saw movement. Was that something long, with hundreds of legs, scampering up that tree, did it have long sharp horns?

Her mind raced and started to play tricks on her.

"I think it's a Milli-molar!" said Tilly.

"A what?" asked Katelyn spinning around.

The clicking started again and out of the trees emerged a long, black, armour-plated body with hundreds of legs and a stag beetle head with two sharp, talon-like horns. It stopped when it saw Tilly and stared at her with its small, sharp black eyes.

It rammed the horns on its head into the ground, and then dragged its head into the air sending the dirt flying. The mouth opened exposing row upon row of small, sharp white teeth.

"I guess that's why they call it a Milli-Molar," whispered Katelyn, visibly shaking in her boots.

"When I say run, you run!" Tilly told Katelyn.

The Milli-Molar lunged forward and covered the ground between itself and Tilly in almost a second.

"RUN!"

Tilly shot into the sky and dropped down onto the creature's back, grabbing the two horns that grew from its head and pulling on them. The creature tried to unseat the little fairy but she held on.

The clicking sound was very loud as the armour plates on its body rubbed against each other. It tried to roll onto its back but Tilly held firm.

The fairy opened her bag and quickly produced a string of dental floss. Unwinding it she tied the floss to the horns and the other end to her little pin.

Katelyn did not run as she was told, instead, she charged towards Scarlett and Charlie and proceeded to claw at the sticky slime that held her two friends in place.

The thick jelly oozed between her fingers as she tried to remove it. She shouted at the pair to wake up and shook them violently.

"Where am I?" asked Scarlett as she slowly awoke. Charlie held his head with his hand, then wished he hadn't because the slime became stuck in his hair.

"This is just not my day, my head hurts," he said.

"You can wash when we get back, we need to run now before we all become lunch!" shouted Katelyn as she pulled at her friends.

"Katelyn, is that you?" asked Scarlett, her eyes spinning in her head as she swayed on the spot.

"Who else would it be? This stuff is like treacle!" grumbled Katelyn as she tried her best to free her friends from the slime.

Meanwhile, not far away the battle was still raging.

"You will not beat me for I am TILLY THE MILLI-MOLAR TAMER!" shouted Tilly as loud as she could. The monster was not ready for defeat yet and tried to drive the two horns into her body. She rolled along the ground to escape the sharp barbs that dared to spear her.

"NOT TODAY!" she cried and sprang up quickly.

Pulling hard on the dental floss, she gritted her teeth as the beast reared its horned head and threw her high into the air like a rag doll.

It twisted its long body around and tried to trap the little fairy but Tilly had a plan and was not scared.

She leapt into the air and then shot like an arrow to the ground, stabbing the pin and the tied dental floss into the earth as deep as she could.

The Milli-Molar reared up and clicked loudly, but it could not break free from the strong floss binding.

Tilly smiled as the beast fought against the tether.

"I've still got it, like old times!" she said to herself.

Katelyn held her stuck friend's hands and pulled as hard as she could until finally out they came with such force that all three fell on top of each other.

"Where are we?" asked Charlie, rubbing his eyes.

"What happened? Katelyn, how did you get here?" said a bleary-eyed Scarlett.

"Will you lot please start running!" shouted Tilly.

They didn't need to be told twice and the little trio ran back through the forest towards the camp. Tilly flew up into the air again and pulled her pin out of the ground, freeing the Milli-Molar.

It scampered back into the forest away from the group, thankfully in the other direction.

"And that's why you don't mess with a tooth fairy!" shouted Tilly after it, and she sheathed her pin and dusted herself off, then flew after the others.

Back at camp the group was clearing up the pots and pans and preparing to leave.

Pippa, Timoir, and Stanley all looked up as they returned at the strange, little group of green-coated children, but said nothing.

"I hope Stanley's craft has a decent shower as I am going to spend a week in there!" said Charlie.

"Thank you for coming after us," whispered Scarlett to Katelyn. "You are a true friend, just don't tell anyone I sounded all mushy. Deal?" she said.

"Deal!" whispered Katelyn back.

Nobody mentioned the events in the forest after that. A lesson had been learned that day.

CHAPTER TWENTY-EIGHT
The Crescent City

The Crescent City was well named for if you were to fly overhead it would resemble a half-moon. It had been established as a trading port many years ago because of its location, bordering the ocean that ran along the Enamel Coast and the Desert of Lost Wisdom.

This meant that it had become the last major city before the trade caravans trekked across the desert or set sail, and subsequently attracted everyone from pixies to gnomes, sprites, fairies, and gremlins.

It was one of the few places to not have an active tooth collection service, however, it did sport a melting pot of musical styles from all of the realms.

One such musical tavern was the Composite Crown, which not only served the best food and drink in town but also attracted the best musicians to its stage.

However, the small group of huddled individuals, who sat around the small table towards the back of the tavern, were not there for the live jazz that played out on the stage.

"So, let me be getting this straight then," said the small gnome, who sat opposite three hooded figures, one of whom was holding an egg. "You want me and my crew to help you capture this Tooth Bearer girl, and stop this flying vessel that her crew is chasing your beloved Toothsayer on. Not only can we keep what we find on-board the ship, but you'll also pay us for our trouble?"

Sharpclaw withdrew his hood and sat back in his chair, flanked on either side by Lenny and Pichael, and clasped his claws together on his chest, smiling the kind of smile only a gremlin can pull off.

"I can see why you are the captain of The Raven, Mister Crowe," he said.

The gnome scowled until his eyes almost disappeared under thick, bushy eyebrows. Although short for a gnome, he was very intimidating in his dark red uniform with gold braid on his shoulders and a three corner pirate hat, known as a Tricorne, sat on his head. He rested his hand on the curved sword that hung at his side. The blade of the scimitar gleamed in the dark shadows of the tavern.

"That's Captain Crowe to you. Captain Christopher Crowe and the crew of The Raven don't come cheap!" the gnome, angered by the gremlin, slammed his tankard onto the table, spilling his honey milk.

Although quick to anger, Captain Crowe had made himself quite a reputation over the years as a feared pirate of the sea and desert. Luckily his temper was quenched by his first mate, a sprite known as Carver, who sat beside him.

"What would you be offering us then as payment? We'd like to see gold on the table," asked Carver.

"Well then. Show our good guests here what we have, Lenny. This is far better than any gold coin!" said Sharpclaw, still smiling broadly, displaying rows of sharp teeth.

Lenny opened up a leather bag and produced a pair of blue fluffy dice held together by a piece of string. He placed them carefully onto the table for all to see as if they were precious gems.

"Gamblers' winning dice. You roll any number and if you don't like it, you just pull the string and roll it to another number without anyone seeing!" Sharpclaw said, demonstrating to the captain by pulling the string. The fluffy dice bounced along the wooden table and rolled to a double six.

"Marvellous, capital idea. What say you Mister Carver?" asked Captain Crowe.

"It's like magic, never seen anything like it!"

Pichael clapped his clawed hand over his face in embarrassment, trying hard not to laugh.

"Well Mister Sharpclaw, it looks like you have hired yourself a ship!" laughed Crowe, and he pocketed the dice.

A small, female fairy wearing a bandana entered and walked over to the group.

"Janice, have we got something to show you!" said the Captain.

"Cap'n, you wanted me to tell you if I saw anything new coming into town. Well, I was at the docks, and I saw this flying boat land in the port. A girl matching the description of the Tooth Bearer was on board!"

"Good show Janice. Well Mister Sharpclaw, it seems your contract has arrived on time. We shall endeavour to stop them as soon as we have captured this Tooth Bearer girl. Alert the crew, Mister Carver, make sail as soon as we see the flying boat leave these shores!" cried Captain Crowe as he stood up and drew his sword, which he waved in the air and proclaimed to all.

"I shall deliver this 'Tooth Bearer' to your very claws by the end of the day. Mark my words!"

"I shall await your call with excited expectation!" replied Sharpclaw.

"This doesn't seem fair, Uncle Lenny. She's just a little girl. What is the Toothsayer going to do with her?" asked Pichael with genuine concern.

"Not for us to question the Toothsayer lad, anyway she is a dangerous girl. She beat Sharpclaw twice!" said Lenny, luckily out of earshot of his mate.

The trio pulled their hoods over their heads and headed to the docks where they saw a crowd gathering. Word had travelled fast of the Tooth Bearer's arrival and many local dignitaries had turned out to greet the group.

"We can't get close with all these people about!" snapped Sharpclaw.

CHAPTER TWENTY-NINE
Missing...

The Mayor of the Crescent City strode out ahead of the group to greet the little girl that had saved them from the Darkness of Disbelief once before and was now risking everything to do it again.

"Greetings brave travellers. I am Mayor Maurice, and I bid you all a warm welcome to The Crescent City. We are all at your disposal whilst you stay here!"

Mayor Maurice was a small gnome with a grey moustache. He was weighed down by the heavy, golden chains of office and red, velvet robes that they were forced to wear. On his head sat a blue velvet flat cap with the official badge of the Crescent City, a half-moon that symbolised the city's shape. The Mayor held out his hand for the first person off the vessel to shake.

"Thank you, Mayor Maurice, we will not be staying long I'm afraid in your fine city. We just require supplies and freshwater before we continue across the desert on our mission," said Toothsayer Timoir as she departed the craft and took the mayor's hand in hers.

"I'm sure we will have time to take in some jazz and a drink or two though, come on Charlie!" said Stanley as he jogged past the pair and headed into the city without a second glance at the other dignitaries who were standing with hands outstretched, hoping someone would shake them.

"Yes, of course. I will make arrangements for anything you need," said Mayor Maurice.

Timoir turned around to the remaining group of friends and said, "Please everyone, we really cannot stay long. Do not get lost and be back here at five to six. The desert is harsh and unforgiving and I wish to cross it whilst we still have light. Charlie, you and I will go and fetch Stanley back again. We cannot afford to lose him," she said.

Katelyn appeared on deck and a great cheer erupted from the crowd, with many people throwing their hats into the air.

"Do not think for a minute that we are going to do that when we are back in school!" said Scarlett, with a slight hint of jealousy in her voice.

"Well I think it is nice and respectful," said Pippa, as she emerged from below decks with Tilly, and waved to the crowd.

"I didn't ask for any of this," replied Katelyn, somewhat embarrassed by the treatment.

"Nobody has ever cheered me. If they did I'd enjoy it, so don't tell me you aren't enjoying the attention Katelyn!" said Scarlett.

"It is nice, I guess. They are cheering us all though, not just me Scarlett," Katelyn said.

Scarlett turned around and stared at the crowds.

"I wish I was a Tooth Bearer," said Scarlett under her breath, however, Katelyn heard her.

"Scarlett, don't be like that. I didn't know I was a Tooth Bearer until I ended up here," said Katelyn.

"Well, I am going to get some pictures with my camera," she sang and skipped down the gangplank that had been placed beside the craft for everyone to easily disembark.

"Scarlett, wait. Don't get lost. I'm coming as well!" said Katelyn, and raced after her friend, who had already dived into the crowd. "I can't believe she did it again!" said Katelyn to herself. No matter where she looked, she couldn't see Scarlett anywhere.

"Scarlett, where have you gone?" she shouted.

Several gnomes and fairies came over to her for a chat and an autograph, and she was soon pulled along with a throng of happy people.

"Wait, I need to find my friend!" she said, as she

was pulled along with the crowd.

"Well, so much for 'Stay here and don't get lost!'" said Pippa, turning to Tilly with a 'why do I bother' expression on her face.

Tilly shrugged her shoulders and feigned a smile, unsure of how to answer. She could remember a time when she was young and craved adventure. How many times had she gone against her aunt's wishes? Too many to mention, she thought to herself.

"Come on, let's go with them. They are only children, and someone needs to keep them out of trouble!" smiled Tilly, as she walked down the boarding plank into the crowd.

"Katelyn, don't worry. I'll go and find Scarlett again. You stay here and suffer writer's cramp from signing your name!" laughed Tilly.

"Oh, the trappings of fame. I'll stay with her and help. Yes, that's right, Pippa is spelt with a 'P'," said Aunt Pippa to a young pixie that had just thrust his autograph book into her hands.

Meanwhile, Scarlett stood amongst the crowd taking pictures with her camera of the buildings. The crowd jostled and barged into her and she was pulled further away from her friends.

"Sign this please, pretty Princess!" said a hopeful

young fairy with a big smile on her face, holding an autograph book out for Scarlett to sign.

"Of course I will, but I'm not the Tooth Bearer. I'm just Scarlett," she said, signing her name.

"But you are helping the Tooth Bearer save us. That makes you a hero to us all!" said the little fairy.

Scarlett stopped writing for a second, she hadn't thought about it like that.

"Being a good friend and helping those in need. That will always make you special!" continued the fairy and danced away into the crowd, clutching the autograph book close to her chest.

Scarlett was only a few metres away from Katelyn, but it could have been a mile. The city had many different styles of architecture because so many different people lived there. It brought something from everyone to its design. It was alive and vibrant, and Scarlett loved it.

"It's a whole new world, and I never knew it existed!" she lamented to herself and turned around trying to spot her friends. All she saw though was the crowd. There must have been at least over a hundred fairies, gnomes, pixies, sprites, and a few gremlins, milling around the docks.

"Whoops, I've gone and got lost again!" she said.

"Hello, you look like you've travelled far, are you lost?" said a female voice from somewhere.

Scarlett turned around to see where the voice was coming from, but there was nobody there.

She walked over to a small alleyway and peeped down the dark passage but couldn't see a thing.

"Hello, did someone say something?" she asked.

"Hello, I asked if you had travelled far?" repeated the voice, and with that, a small fairy, wearing a bandana and holding a coin which she casually tossed into the air and caught without a second glance, flew down into the alley and landed gracefully in front of Scarlett.

"Hello, my name is Janice. Are you the Tooth Bearer that I have heard so much about?" the fairy asked.

"Well, I'll need a receipt, but you can have my autograph. I wish I was the Tooth Bearer but...!" she started to say, but was interrupted by Janice.

"No autograph, but I know someone that wants to meet you!" and quick as a flash the fairy threw a sack over Scarlett and tied it up. Scarlett kicked out but to no avail. She was trapped.

"Hey, not fair. Let me out!" cried the sack.

"I have her Mister Sharpclaw, I told you I could do it!" Janice shouted gleefully.

"Excellent work Janice, tell your Captain Crowe to take care of the others," the gremlin said, appearing from the shadows. He grabbed the sack and tossed it over his back.

"Please let me out. HELP ME!" shouted the sack.

"Hey boss, you look like that bloke that breaks into humans' houses once a year, and eats mince pies!" laughed Lenny.

"HO, HO, HO!" mocked Sharpclaw.

"Mister Sharpclaw, this isn't fair. Let her out," cried Pichael, pulling at the sack.

"HELP, let me out this minute!" shouted the sack.

"Not being fair is not being cured by the Molten Moonlight Potion. This little girl will give me back my freedom," snapped Sharpclaw.

"But Mister Sharpclaw!" started Pichael.

"Cake Tin has been a thorn in my side since I first met her. Well, enough is enough!" snapped the gremlin.

"But...,"

"Enough Pichael, we are already on our chosen path. Now open up that magic door!" he snapped.

"Come on Pichael. When you are older you will understand!" said Lenny, as he helped Sharpclaw carry the sack.

"Ouch, I am really angry now so let me out!" shouted Scarlett from within the sack.

"Toothsayer Tiana will be so pleased to see you, Tooth Bearer!" said Lenny to the sack.

"Hang on, there has been a mistake!" said the sack.

"Pichael, the door please, and today would be nice!" said Sharpclaw.

Pichael put down his egg and placed the door onto the floor. It glowed around the edges and light shone through the keyhole.

"Quick, before Tills and her friends arrive!"

Just then Tilly came around the corner and spotted the gremlins and the wriggling, Scarlett-shaped sack.

"Sharpclaw and Lenny. What a surprise seeing you here. How is your new mistress these days?" asked Tilly.

"Well, well, well. If it isn't Tills again. We do keep meeting up in the most unusual places, don't we?" Sharpclaw mocked the little fairy.

"What have you got there in that sack?" Tilly asked.

"Wouldn't you like to know? This time she won't be coming to save you with her torch!" smiled Sharpclaw, and he opened the magic door letting the magic light of the portal stream out, illuminating the alley in bright yellow light.

"Help me please!" screamed the sack.

Lenny pushed Pichael through the door and helped Sharpclaw throw the sack after him.

"Stop, let her out!" shouted Tilly and ran forwards.

"Tilly, is that you? HELP ME!" shouted the sack from the other side of the door.

The fairy ran towards them, but tripped over something and fell onto her face, skidding to a stop.

"Ouch, that hurt!" she said as she climbed to her feet and rubbed her sore shins.

"HA, HA, HA!" laughed Sharpclaw.

"Nice try Tooth Fairy, but you are too late!" cried Lenny as tears of laughter rolled down his cheeks.

"Such a pity, little Tills. So clumsy. How on earth did you ever become a tooth fairy?" jeered Sharpclaw as he and Lenny crossed the threshold, laughing as they went.

The door slammed shut and locked itself, leaving Tilly in the dirt. With the door now locked, the link between doors was broken.

Tilly got up and dusted herself down, and looked at her feet. Bending down she picked up the cause of her stumble. It was a large, warm egg with the name 'NANCY' written on it in pen.

It was covered in drawings of trains, drawings of a grumpy Toothsayer Tiana, pictures of Sharpclaw and Lenny, and a map of a forest with the letter 'X', scrawled onto a drawing of a clearing, all mixed in with pictures of cakes and strange muddy giants wearing doilies on their heads.

"Where have you gone?" she asked herself.

CHAPTER THIRTY

The Raven

"Everybody, let us just please keep calm. We will make haste and rescue Scarlett. Trust me, we will get her back!" said Toothsayer Timoir, when everyone had gathered back at the Spirit of Landon.

"It was all my fault, I should have tried harder to catch her!" said Katelyn.

"Scarlett is a strong girl, Katelyn. It was nobody's fault," Timoir stated bluntly.

"We have stocked up with water and supplies. Ready to depart when you give the go-ahead," said Stanley.

"They dropped this gremlin egg when they went

through the door. Look, I think someone was drawing a map. Maybe we have someone on their side who will help us?" said Tilly, holding the egg for all to see.

"Ooh, it's like an Easter egg. The drawing of Tiana is quite good," said Pippa, casting her gaze over the pictures.

"Is it made of chocolate?" asked Charlie.

Katelyn gave her friend a sideways glance.

"Heavens no, I'd have eaten it by now if it were. No, I mean it has secret information written on it that will help us find Scarlett!" said Pippa.

"Tilly, you collected the door that the gremlins used to escape through?" asked Timoir.

The little fairy held up the small door for all to see. It had shrunk in size when it closed so Tilly had been able to place it in her bag for safekeeping.

"Good, that may come in handy," said Timoir, as Tilly tried to open the door but failing, placed it back in her bag.

"My sister will have made sure it is magically locked, Tilly. Keep it safe for now, I will have to think of a way to open it," Timoir said thoughtfully.

"Then if we are all ready to go, let us take off. The sooner we cross the desert the better. Charlie, prime the engine and get her boiled up. We are going full steam ahead with no stops," commanded Stanley, as he started turning knobs and pulling levers in the cabin.

The giant balloon that hovered over the cabin expanded as hot air was pumped into it. Charlie, who had decided to learn about the craft as they travelled, was busy pumping a pair of rubber bellows connected to a pressurised boiler, which in turn heated up the boiler causing steam to whoosh through the pipes and power the vessel.

Slowly the Spirit of Landon rose from the docks of the Crescent City into the sky. Even though their visit had been brief the crowds had still turned out to see them go.

Katelyn was up on deck, staring into the distance as if trying to see her lost friend. Timoir came up to stand beside her and placed a friendly hand on her shoulder.

"Scarlett will be alright, I have only known her a short time but I can see she is a brave girl," she said.

"I think they were after me. If only I had seen her in the crowd, I could have helped her!" said Katelyn, with tears in her eyes. "She wanted to be a Tooth Bearer. I'm worried she might have been jealous when we lost each other!"

"We will catch up with her, and rescue her together. Do not blame yourself. A burden such as yours should never have been placed upon the shoulders of one so young. Being a Tooth Bearer is no easy task." Timoir tried to calm the little girl.

The desert opened up before them as they left the lights of the city behind them. Soon the noise of the busy port city vanished as well, to be replaced by the pistons and steam valves of the flying ship.

Charlie came up on deck to stand beside Katelyn and Timoir. He was oil-stained and red-faced but he looked happy. Katelyn smiled when she saw him.

"Hello Katelyn, I came to see how you were?" he said.

"You and Stanley look like two peas in a pod."

"I didn't think I'd enjoy this flying lark but I am. It's very cool," he said.

Charlie sighed when he saw Katelyn's face.

"Scarlett is a tough cookie, Katelyn. I'd hate to be the other person when they open up that sack!" Charlie said with a smile, hoping it would help.

They crossed the desert, gliding over the dunes in good time with the wind at their back. Several hours passed as they flew along and the group kept themselves busy by playing card games or singing songs to cheer everyone up.

The desert seemed devoid of life, and the only thing they saw was the occasional rocky outcrop.

"I would have thought we would have seen another trader at least," commented Stanley.

As the sun started to go down, the comforting whiff of cooking food could be smelt from the galley below. Pippa was baking an apple pie with dandelion spiced raisins for tea.

As Charlie took the helm, Stanley was able to come on deck for a breath of fresh air.

"Why do they call this 'The Desert of Lost Wisdom' then?" asked Katelyn.

"Well, young Katelyn. It is said that anyone who falls overboard and lands in these sandy dunes will sink for all eternity. So to travel across this desert, well, you'd have to be pretty silly," answered Stanley, as he gazed towards the horizon.

"Do you recognise this clearing within a forest, that we saw drawn on the egg?" Timoir asked Stanley.

"Plenty of forests on the other side could be any number of clearings. However, if you say that your sister plans to grow a giant fairy ring, well, it would have to be a pretty big clearing."

"True, I do recall there used to be a village about thirty miles into the forest. Everyone had to leave when the Darkness expanded into the territory. There used to be a huge clearing close to the village. I bet Tiana is headed there," said Timoir.

"If only we could use that magic door, we could go straight to Tiana and rescue Scarlett!" said Katelyn.

The night was drawing in and soon stars started to appear in the night's sky.

Stanley, who had been staring into the horizon, suddenly looked puzzled.

"That's odd, I've navigated by the stars many a time. I have never seen that star before!" he said pointing into the distance.

"It's too low to be a star in the sky!" said Timoir.

"A new moon perhaps?" asked Stanley.

The star got brighter and brighter.

"That's no moon or star, it's coming towards us!" said Katelyn.

"Pirates, I bet!" said Stanley.

"I have a very bad feeling about this, turn the ship around Stanley!" said Timoir.

"Right, hold on!" and he rushed to the wheelhouse to take over from Charlie.

"What's going on?" said Charlie, as he came running over to see the strange light that was gaining on them.

"Better strap yourselves in, it might get rough!" shouted Stanley from the wheelhouse.

"Strap ourselves in. What do you expect us to strap ourselves to?!" asked Pippa as she emerged.

"Do you think it is pirates?" asked Tilly, who had followed Pippa up on deck.

The light continued to get brighter and brighter.

CHAPTER THIRTY-ONE

The battle

"Arrgh, I can't see a thing. That light is too bright!" shouted Stanley, rubbing his eyes.

"Turn the ship around. Charlie, help Stanley in the wheelhouse!" shouted Timoir.

"I can hear someone calling us!" shouted Tilly, as she tried to shield her vision from the blinding light.

"Crew of the Spirit of Landon, prepare to be boarded. You have the honour of being robbed by non-other than Captain Christopher Crowe of the Raven, Hurrah!"

"Who is Christopher Crowe, is he a pirate?" asked Katelyn.

"Only the most feared in all the sand, sea, and air, and he's not getting my ship!" replied Stanley, grabbing the wheel and spinning it around, turning the Spirit of Landon away from the light.

"Excellent, I love a good sport. Makes the adventure more exciting. Crew, ready the ship for battle. Janice, prepare the chase cannon and fire on my command!" shouted the voice from the other ship.

A forward-facing chase cannon was wheeled to the bow of the ship by Janice the fairy.

"Target that ship!" shouted Captain Crowe, from the deck of the Raven.

"Try and catch me!" cried Stanley and he pulled a lever. The Spirit of Landon shot forward, flying over the dunes, smoke billowing out of the steam funnel.

"Stanley, please give us some warning before you fly off like that!" shouted Pippa, as she grabbed a chair and tied herself into it.

The night's sky was lit up as the Spirit flew in front of the Raven, just out of reach.

"Timoir, can you stop them with magic. Maybe a freeze spell or something?" shouted Pippa.

"If the ship was steady enough, and I wasn't in the

driest desert in our realm I might. I need some water in the air to perform ice magic!" shouted Timoir.

"He's gaining on us!" shouted Charlie.

"What is that light, I can hardly see?!" shouted Pippa.

"They seem to have some sort of metal torch strapped to the base of their ship. They must have picked it up in the human realm!" said Timoir, straining to see the approaching ship.

"I think it used to be mine!" said Charlie.

All conversation stopped as a loud BOOM was heard. A bright, green ball of slime flew over the deck and landed on the floor, splattering all.

"SLIME BALLS, take cover!" shouted Stanley.

"Help, I'm covered in goo!" cried Katelyn.

Tilly rushed over and pulled Katelyn to her feet. The deck of the craft was covered in large blobs of green slime that stuck to everything.

BOOM!

Another large ball of slime flew over the ship, narrowly missing the craft as Stanley fought with the wheel, spinning it this way and that.

"Why are they shooting slime at us? I thought

pirates fired cannonballs," shouted Katelyn.

"Why destroy a ship when you can beach it and steal everything. They intend to cover us in so much slime that we won't be able to fly!" shouted Stanley from the wheelhouse.

"Gentlemen, give up and prepare to be boarded at once. You've had your fun!" shouted the Captain from the Raven.

"I don't think they are stopping Cap'n!" said Carver, as he lowered his telescope.

"Well, well, well. Bad sportsmanship is what it is. Don't know when they are out for the count. Fire the chase cannon again, Janice, sink their ship into the desert!" said Captain Crowe.

"Aye, Aye Captain!" cried Janice.

BOOM!

Another ball of slime flew over and hit the Spirit of Landon's huge balloon. It twisted and buckled as the slime slid down the fabric.

Captain Crowe drew his sword and pointed it at the 'Spirit of Landon'.

"I will have that vessel before the sun sets over this desert and the day is through!" he shouted.

"Aye, Aye Captain!" shouted his crew.

Timoir aimed her staff at the bright light and chanted, "Fulmination fireball!"

A flaming ball of fire flew from the tip of her staff, but it went wide and slammed through a sandy dune, blowing the fine grains into the air.

Toothsayer Timoir tried casting the spell again at

the Raven, but she was blinded by the torch hanging from the hull and it fizzled into the sand below.

"She can't take much more of this, another hit on the balloon and we'll go down!" bawled Stanley.

"Can we throw something else at them?" cried Katelyn, desperately trying to hang onto the deck.

"We don't have anything apart from Pippa's apple pies!" Stanley responded bluntly.

"No, don't you even think about it. I slaved all day cooking those," screamed Pippa.

"Wait, I have an idea. I'm sorry Aunt Pippa but it involves your apple pies after all!" said Tilly and she rushed to the galley and piled the apple pies into the oven. She turned up the heat on the stove.

BOOM!

Another ball of slime hit the deck causing everyone to fall on their faces. The craft groaned and moaned as the wood started to split.

"We're going down!" shouted Stanley.

All of a sudden, thick black smoke poured from the funnel and the smell of burning apples filled the air.

The black smoke poured out behind the craft, obscuring the Raven's advance.

"My apple pies!" screeched Pippa.

"Bad sports!" yelled Captain Crowe from the smoke-covered Raven, as the ship disappeared from view into the distance.

"We are not out of the woods yet, the old girl's taken too much damage. I'm going to have to land!" said Stanley.

"We don't have time, we need to rescue Scarlett!" pleaded Katelyn.

"We will Katelyn, I promise you!" said Tilly.

"Look, the edge of the desert and I can see a forest. We made it!" cried a triumphant Charlie.

"Now that just leaves the edge of the Darkness to contend with!" said Timoir, as she pointed towards the area ahead. It was the first time any of the group, except Timoir, had seen the Darkness of Disbelief up close.

The sky was a deep, dark purple colour with swirls of black mist that danced and leapt in the air as if a macabre play was being performed by ghosts. The forest ahead, once green, was now a dark, foreboding, unhappy collection of twisted trees and deep, overgrown vines, grown tightly together in such a way, that you might believe that the forest was trying to keep you out.

The Spirit of Landon came down with a loud crash onto the edge of the forest. The hull cracked open as the craft hit the ground and it slid along, leaving a trail of pots and pans and other contents from the hull in its wake, before coming to a halt against some large rocks.

The huge balloon that had carried them this far now deflated and sank across the funnel and wheelhouse, covering the ship like a veil.

Tilly was the first to emerge from under the deflated balloon. She had a nasty bruise on her face but apart from that, she seemed okay. She held the fabric up to allow Pippa and Stanley, Charlie and Timoir, and finally Katelyn the chance to climb out. Thankfully nobody was hurt.

Stanley stood up and inspected the ship. He patted the old hull as if it was a family pet.

"Don't worry old girl, I'll patch you up and get you flying again," he said.

"What now?" asked Charlie.

"It will take at least a day or two for me to mend this old girl," said Stanley, sadly.

"We don't have time, can we walk from here?"

Tilly had asked the question that nobody wanted to answer. For each of them knew the response.

"If the markings on that egg are correct, then we would have at least another day's walk ahead of us," said Toothsayer Timoir.

Travelling through the Darkness of Disbelief on foot was perilous at the best of times. Timoir would not be able to protect everyone with her magic for that length of time, even if they were marching along.

"We have to do something!" said Pippa angrily.

"Do any traders come this close to the Darkness, we could hitch a ride?" asked Charlie.

"Nobody is silly enough to come here. Everyone that ever lived in this area fled," said Tilly.

Toothsayer Timoir finally stood up. She had an idea, but it was dangerous.

"Tilly, please can I have that magic door from your bag?" she asked.

Tilly rummaged in her satchel whilst Toothsayer Timoir withdrew a white bone wand from her sleeve and inspected it carefully.

"This belonged to my sister. I picked it up when she was at Katelyn's house. There might be enough of Tiana's magic within this wand to allow me to effectively break the lock on the magic door for a very brief time, to allow us through."

"We can go through the door and rescue Scarlett!"

cried Katelyn.

"If it worked, I would only be able to hold the door open for a second, to allow one, or two, to go through. Some would have to remain here!" her voice was sombre as she spoke to the group.

"Those that remain..?" asked Pippa, but her voice trailed away as her throat dried up.

"Those that remain, without protection from either myself or the Tooth Bearer, would start to feel the effects of the Darkness of Disbelief," Timoir said.

Everyone went quiet.

"Toothsayer Timoir, you must stay here and protect the others with your magic until Stanley can repair the ship. I will go through the door and rescue Scarlett and stop Tiana," said Katelyn bravely, though she was shaking with fear.

"You will need a guardian tooth fairy at your side. Count me in as well!" said Tilly, jumping up.

"Me as well!" said Charlie.

"No Charlie, you must stay here and help Stanley fix the ship, he needs your help!" said Katelyn.

"Katelyn...," said Toothsayer Timoir.

"Toothsayer, you told me earlier that the burden should never have been laid on the shoulders of one so young. Well, it will soon be my birthday, and I will be nine years old. I think that's old enough to take on the burden. You need to stay here and protect the others from the Darkness. I can do this because I know that I have you all looking out for me!" the little girl said.

Toothsayer Timoir closed her eyes and nodded.

"Alright," she said.

"You make sure that you come back to us!" said Pippa. Although she sounded stern, her voice quaked with fear and she fought back the tears.

"We will be waiting for you, Tooth Bearer," said Stanley the gnome.

Toothsayer Timoir placed the wand into the lock on the magic door and closed her eyes.

Bright blue sparks flared from the wand and lit the door up as she turned it slowly in the lock. The door tried to resist but Timoir kept pushing. Every wooden notch and line on the little door burst with bright blue flames, and the door flew open. The Toothsayer kept the wand in place, jammed in the lock, for if she released it the door would slam shut.

"Go now, I can't hold it for long!" Timoir shouted, she sounded strained from the magic that flew down the wand into the door like lightning.

Tilly jumped over the magic threshold, closely followed by Katelyn. Neither of them knew where the magic door led. It was a leap of faith.

"Come back to us, please!" cried Pippa.

They looked back at each other one last time, just as Timoir pulled the wand free.

The door slammed shut.

The blue flame extinguished.

Silence returned.

CHAPTER THIRTY-TWO

The Masked Crown

It took Scarlett a minute to realise what was happening. She couldn't see anything through the heavy sack and it smelt of mouldy vegetables.

"Ouch!"

"You don't need to throw me. I'm sorry, there has been a mistake..., wait, I know that voice!" exclaimed Scarlett. "Tilly, is that you? HELP ME!" she shouted.

It was dark inside the sack, but then, all of a sudden..., a blinding light erupted all around her.

"Arrgh, the light is really bright, what is happening to me? Was that a door closing, am I in a building now?" she asked herself.

"Tilly, are you there still, hello..., anyone?"

Nobody answered the trapped little girl.

"Great, well done Scarlett. Pride before a fall, as my dad tells me, and I've fallen well and truly over my pride," she told herself. "Hello, is there anybody there?"

Although she couldn't see anything, the bright light that had flashed suddenly had left her seeing spots. She knew that she wasn't in the Crescent City anymore because the stone floor beneath her now felt cold to the touch through the sack, and for some reason, it also seemed to be vibrating, as if in motion. Like a train feels when it is travelling along the tracks.

The sack was pulled open and light spilt inside, two rough claws grabbed her arms and pulled upwards, lifting her into the air.

"Eh, boss. This ain't the Tooth Bearer, it's that red-haired friend of hers!" said Lenny.

"What do you mean, it must be her?!" said Sharpclaw, as he pushed Lenny to one side and stared at the girl.

"What are you doing in the sack?!" he said in a startled voice.

"Why don't you tell me!" said an angry Scarlett.

"But, I thought..., Tooth Bearer, I heard Tooth Bearer!" Sharpclaw stuttered.

"Who is the pretty lady, Uncle?" asked Pichael.

"I've never seen her before, but it ain't the Tooth Bearer!" said Lenny in wide-eyed shock.

"I'm Scarlett, and I demand that you take me back to the city and my friends!"

"Miss, you don't demand anything!" snarled Sharpclaw, as he glared at the girl.

Pichael looked shocked and lost.

"UNCLE, I lost Nancy! I must have dropped her in the street!" he cried, frantically searching the floor and rapping on the locked magical door.

"I'm done for, that's it, Sharpclaw, go dig me a hole to lay in. If Toothsayer Tiana doesn't do me in, my Sister will, now I've gone and lost Nancy!" said Lenny, sitting on the floor and rocking to and fro.

"Tills was there, I'm sure she would have picked up Nancy. She might be a pain in the bum but she does try and help folk she meets," said Sharpclaw.

CLAP, CLAP, CLAP!

They all turned around as one, to see Toothsayer Tiana walking towards them, clapping her hands and smiling. It was her smile that unnerved them.

"You really are comedy gold, Sharpclaw, and Lenny. I tell you, if I wasn't looking to claim the realm, I would be a theatre agent and book the pair of you."

"Eh, I'm lost. Are you happy or sad?" asked Sharpclaw.

Lenny and Pichael slowly edged backwards, expecting the worst.

"Neither, I mean, I should be angry with you, but you all make me laugh so much, and I have so missed laughing these past few years. Now run along before I try a few new spells out on you. Leave the girl here!" said Tiana, and dismissively waved her hand.

The gremlins didn't need to be told twice and scampered away as quickly as they could, their tails between their legs.

Toothsayer Tiana looked towards Scarlett, her eyes examining the little girl carefully.

"Are you afraid of me, child?" asked Tiana quietly.

"I want to go home!" said Scarlett nervously.

"As do we all, my child. Now come closer, so that I may have a better view of you."

Scarlett walked slowly forward, she felt like the floor had become smeared with glue, with every step becoming harder and harder.

"That's it, child. Come closer into the light."

"Where am I?" asked Scarlett.

"You are aboard the royal train, in my tower"

Scarlett looked about the room in shock. It was at least forty metres round with an open fireplace that warmed the room as it crackled and spat flames. Pictures hung on the stone walls and a desk, overflowing with scrolls sat in one corner. Bookcases lined the walls and an open window faced a dark purple sky, which swirled with dark shapes that looked vaguely human in form.

"How can we be on a train?" Scarlett asked, she screwed up her face as she tried to take it all in.

"Perception deceives reality," said Tiana. "This tower is part of the train, but in here, it is my realm. This is where I lived for years whilst I remained within the Darkness of Disbelief. The tower is vast inside, yet outside stands only about ten metres tall," said Tiana, and she pointed to an opening in the wall where a purple sky could be seen.

"Look out the window, my child," she said.

Scarlett did as she was told. Outside a giant mound of earth seemed to be moving slowly in a large circle. Every now and again a part of the mound would drop off and land on the ground. As the hulking mound moved the bits that had fallen off grew into large, crystal-encrusted mushrooms.

"That is Eartha, my golem. It is planting the seeds for the future of this realm. Once the ring is completed it will pull in all the humans that step into a fairy ring to this spot. My loyal subjects, ready to do my bidding. Just like Eartha," said Tiana smiling.

"You can't kidnap people. That's illegal and it's wrong" said Scarlett.

"What is the first thing you remember?" asked Tiana.

"I don't know. My dad working hard, the colour purple. Newspapers perhaps?" said Scarlett.

"Purple?" said Tiana.

"I've always liked the colour, I don't know why?"

"Purple like the sky," said the Toothsayer.

Toothsayer Tiana stood over Scarlett and looked down at the little red-haired girl. She put her hand on Scarlett's shoulder and held her firmly.

"The first time that I saw you, I felt as if we had met before, but how could we have?" she exclaimed. "Tell me, what does your father do for a living?"

"He works and owns a paper shop," said Scarlett.

"How quaint, and I take it he is working hard to afford a more, structurally complete building?"

"I don't understand?" questioned Scarlett.

"Open your mouth child. Show me your teeth!"

Scarlett did as she was told and opened her mouth.

"One set is all you get," said Tiana smiling, she seemed to know more than she was letting on. "All these years, and I never once expected to see you again. You never questioned why your skin always glowed with a healthy sheen. Why you have never lost a tooth!" Tiana proclaimed.

"I really have no idea what you're talking about!" answered Scarlett, feeling nervous.

"Look to your past, child. Reach into your heart and see the truth that is burnt into your very being!"

"I...," said Scarlett.

"My child, you are the lost daughter of King Pontin. The baby girl that I sent away with her father, the King of this realm all those years ago!" Tiana proclaimed holding her arms out wide.

"No, you lie!" shouted Scarlett angrily.

"You grew up, never knowing the past that you had left behind. My magic worked well in protecting you all. The glamour spell that I cast upon your body grew alongside you. You truly think that you are human!" the Toothsayer said.

"I want to go home now!" said Scarlett.

"You are home, this is your kingdom!"

Toothsayer Tiana waved her hand over Scarlett's head and the red-haired girl glowed with a bright yellow light. Her skin, which had glowed with the glamour spell for nine years changed to a silvery sheen. Fine silken wings sprouted from her back and lay folded, unused, beside her waist. Her red hair sparkled with thousands of silvery pearls.

"HELP ME!" Scarlett shouted and fell to her knees.

Toothsayer Tiana bowed with regal grace.

"My little Princess, I have missed you so!" she said.

Scarlett looked up and sobbed, her wings folded around her body, which shook as her tears fell.

Tiana held out her hand and Scarlett took it, allowing herself to be lifted to her feet.

"Join me, my Princess. Let us rule this world together, as it should have been. The masked crown unveiled and restored to the throne," Tiana said triumphantly.

"I..., I don't know what to do. I want to see my

friends. I want my dad. I want to see Katelyn and Charlie again. This is wrong, I'm not a fairy!" Scarlett said angrily, but in her heart, she knew the truth. She could not deny her wings.

"We are what we are, my child, but I will let you decide. I will send for Mister Beeching to make up a room for you. Make no mistake, you are our missing princess. Daughter of King Pontin and heir to the throne of Landon!" Tiana said, bowing once more through tear-stained eyes.

"And I am your Toothsayer and you're my...,"

The words failed her for the first time in years.

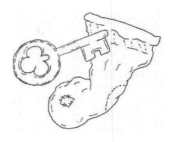

CHAPTER THIRTY-THREE

Chains broken and free

Pichael walked the halls of the tower with a fearful frown.

He had lost his sister, and right now he was not living up to the expected ideals of being a gremlin.

Living the life of a gremlin was no easy task. Most of the continent distrusted you for starters, hiding their belongings as soon as you appeared or blaming you for things that happened in the human realm like stealing an odd sock.

Most of that last one was true, to be honest.

If something like a red sock ended up in the wash mixed with white clothes or your car keys disappeared, then it was usually a gremlin up to no good.

All gremlins were trained from an early age to be mischievous, and it was seen as a balance in the chaos that is the universe. The tooth fairy provided a service and the gremlin provided a disservice.

Could you break the mould and do something unexpected for a gremlin?

He snarled to himself, wondering if he should 'thumb his tooth' at Tiana, and stomp over her mushroom patch. She was so grumpy!

He passed a solid-looking wooden door and heard crying from the other side. He stopped and knocked with his claw.

"Hello, are you alright?" he asked.

"Why would you care?" came the response.

"Well, you are locked in a very tiny room and it is not much fun in there on your own," he replied.

"What has that got to do with the price of a daily paper," came the reply.

"Because I'm such a fungi and you are locked in such a tiny room, there's not mushroom in there!" laughed Pichael at his bad joke.

"What, do you think that this is funny?!"

"Well I'm a fungi, you know, I'm such a fun guy!"

Scarlett wasn't in the mood for jokes however and kept silent. The only audience for the little gremlin it would seem was the closed wooden door.

"My name is Pichael, what do they call you?" he asked, trying a different tactic.

"Scarlett Dorsey. At least I think that's my real name. After today, I'm not so sure!"

"Can I come in?" he asked.

"Sure, but it's locked, you know that," came the blunt reply.

"If I open it, will you help me find my sister?" asked the little gremlin.

"What does she look like?" asked Scarlett from behind the door.

"Well, at the moment she looks like an egg. She hasn't hatched yet!" he said.

"An egg?!" said Scarlett.

"I'm a gremlin, we come from eggs!" replied Pichael.

"Then she is as stuck in her egg as I am in this room. Unless you have the key for the lock!" replied Scarlett bluntly.

"I'm born for locks!" said Pichael happily, and quickly went to work on the door lock. He prodded the lock with his claw, and soon the welcoming sound of a click occurred, and the door opened.

"She really did put you in the smallest room in the tower, not mushroom in here at all!" he smiled as he entered.

"What are you, Tiana's comic clown? It wasn't funny the first time!" Scarlett stated, climbing off the small bed she had been sitting on.

"I'm trying to cheer you up!" said Pichael.

"Well, get some better jokes for starters," she said.

Pichael stared at Scarlett in her new form for the first time.

"Wow, you really are the fairy princess!" exclaimed Pichael as he stared at the red-haired girl, with delicate fairy wings sprouting from her back.

"I know, have a laugh!" said Scarlett angrily.

"I'm not laughing, I like your wings. Why are you locked in here?" he asked.

"I am to be made Queen of the realm if I join with Tiana," said Scarlett.

"Wow, the world is your oyster, but locked in this small room, the oyster is your world," said Pichael.

"Yeah..., okay," said Scarlett.

"So are you going to tell me your story?" asked Pichael, jumping up onto the bed.

"Toothsayer Tiana wants me to join her in taking over this world and rule the humans she kidnaps. So she locked me in this room until I decide what I want to do, but she isn't telling me everything. I know that she is hiding something. I want to go home!" finished Scarlett sadly.

"Sounds like you have made up your mind already."

"I don't think I have a choice in what I want to do!" Scarlett said gloomily.

"Break the mould!" said Pichael.

"Pardon?" asked Scarlett.

"You're a princess, and expected to rule. So break the mould and do what you want to do!"

"I want to see my dad, and go home," she said.

"Then break the mould and go home to your dad. Stuff ruling the world!" exclaimed Pichael.

"Stuff the mushrooms!" laughed Scarlett. "Break the mould, I like it..., first though, I'm going to break up that horrid mushroom ring and stop your Toothsayer!" she said smiling at the little gremlin, who smiled a toothy grin back.

"My way of thinking, I'll help!" said Pichael.

CHAPTER THIRTY-FOUR
The rescue from fear

Elsewhere, at around the same time, in the main hall, a small, magical fairy door started to glow with a bright light that illuminated the wooden frame.

It glowed brighter.

Brighter still.

The door burst open, light streamed through the opening, and over the threshold jumped Tilly Lightfeather and Katelyn.

"Oh my, I did not expect this!" said Tilly, as she stared at her surroundings.

"Where do you think we are?" asked Katelyn.

"Nowhere I wish to be, that's for sure," replied her

friend, as she examined the bookshelves and desk.

"What do you suppose this is for?" asked Tilly, picking up a small, earthen statue.

"Someone collects really ugly dolls, that's for sure!" said Katelyn.

"Look, a bag of teeth and they're warm!" said Tilly.

"Are we in a castle?" asked Katelyn.

"We seem to be in a stone tower. Look out of the window!" said a shocked Tilly.

Katelyn ran to the open window and peered out. The sky was a deep purple colour with swirls of dark black clouds. A forest surrounded the tower with twisted, blackened trees. Upon the ground, beneath the tower was a giant, unfinished circle of mushrooms. A slow-moving mound of earth, roughly human-shaped ambled along leaving a trail of sprouting mushrooms in its wake. The circle was nearly complete.

"It's a tower and a train!" exclaimed Katelyn.

"I think we are in the right place. Those mushrooms are our target. If we destroy the circle, then Tiana won't be able to bring the humans through!" said Tilly pointing at the circle. "We'd better destroy it soon, it's nearly finished!"

"As are you, my fine-tooth collector!" said Tiana,

coming in, with Mister Beeching, through a side door in the tower wall.

"Did you expect to win so easily? I knew you'd try to stop me. One reason I stole the Tooth Bearer teeth was to alert me to your approach!" She held up her fist and chanted, "Glaciate benumb!"

Immediately ice formed in the palm of her hand. With her other hand, she held a tooth. It was a Tooth Bearer tooth, and she proceeded to touch the ice with it. The ice immediately melted, and water trickled between her fingers.

"Tooth Bearer teeth get warmer as the Tooth Bearer gets closer. You know that, little fairy. From experience, I believe!" Tiana coldly said.

Tilly remembered her first meeting with Katelyn, which seemed so long ago now.

"It is so nice that you arrived, and I must congratulate your ingenuity on using my own, locked fairy door as an entry portal. Tell me, is my dear sister here as well, I seem to have dropped my wand someplace?" asked Tiana.

Katelyn and Tilly scowled at the Toothsayer.

"You won't win, I'm going to stop you!" shouted Katelyn, clenching her fists in anger.

"Of course you are. Small girl tries against the odds

and defeats the evil witch. Only trouble is, little Tooth Bearer, this isn't a fairy story!"

Katelyn and Tilly turned to one another and said in unison, "Well, it kind of is a fairy story!"

"Very funny, I see we have a double act to entertain us," mocked Tiana.

She placed the tooth inside a bag on the table next to the ugly statue and pointed a finger at the pair.

"Gelatine pulp engulf" shouted Tiana and pointed a finger at Tilly and Katelyn. Green light streamed towards the pair, hitting them squarely in their chest, and immediately the light expanded to surround them in green, sticky slime. They were stuck fast and couldn't move.

"Mister Beeching, please put the fairy outside the tower. Let's see how long it takes her to forget who she is!" said Tiana.

"Are you sure, Toothsayer? The Darkness will rob her of mind and soul without magic for protection," replied the sprite.

"I am well aware of what the Darkness will do, Mister Beeching. Proceed."

The sprite sighed and rolled the fairy towards the tower exit.

Toothsayer Tiana turned her attention towards the

trapped Tooth Bearer and stared at her with cold, steel grey eyes.

She smiled, but it wasn't warming or friendly at all.

"As for you, little girl. I know I can't change your mind, but maybe you will get some enjoyment from seeing your fellow humans appear. I hear all you lost children have caused quite a stir back in the human realm. Lots of people searching for you. So neighbourly of them. It almost brings a tear to my eye. You simply must remind me to thank them, when they start to appear through my fairy ring!"

Katelyn struggled, but it was to no avail. She could do nothing but watch as her friend was taken away.

Mister Beeching rolled the large orb of solid green slime that contained Tilly, towards the main door of the tower. Opening it, he pushed Tilly outside into the Darkness of Disbelief. "Sorry little one, it's nothing personal," he said.

Meanwhile, Pichael and Scarlett crept along the hallways. The tower seemed to be a maze, with one corridor leading into another, then back on itself.

"We will never get out, I'm sure I've passed this painting before!" moaned Scarlett.

"Yes, we will. Gremlins always find a way!" replied Pichael.

"Hold up Pichael, what are you doing?" said a familiar voice.

Turning, the pair faced Sharpclaw and Lenny.

"Uncle, I'm setting Scarlett free. This is all wrong. You know it, I know it and even Mister Sharpclaw knows it!" shouted Pichael, with bravery that astonished even himself.

"Pichael, if we don't help Tiana, then Sharpclaw turns into a statue again. He needs the Molten Moonlight potion that she holds," Lenny reminded his nephew.

"No, he doesn't because I have it here. I swiped it off the table when I stole some cake. When we first saw that golem on the train!" said Pichael, throwing the warm potion bottle over to Sharpclaw, who caught it easily.

"Pichael, I don't know what to say!" said Sharpclaw, as he emptied the contents over his body. The burning liquid was quickly absorbed into his scaly skin, which reverted to its original green colour.

"You can say 'Let's get out of here and go find my sister', for one," said Pichael.

"When did you grow up, Nephew?" asked Lenny.

"I think he's earned his crystal tooth, what you say, Lenny?" remarked Sharpclaw.

"Yes, definitely. He's as devious as his old dad was!" said Lenny.

"Right, if you three have finished bonding and having the group hugs, we need to escape and destroy that fairy ring!" commanded Scarlett.

"Why should we help you? We have our own crystal teeth. If we wanted, we could leave right now. So what's to stop us, Princess?" asked Sharpclaw.

"Yeah, we have what we want. What's to stop us!" said Lenny, backing up Sharpclaw.

Pichael stamped his foot on the stone floor in anger and stammered, "We are going to help Scarlett. We have to destroy the ring because..., because if we don't all the humans will be here, instead of there, and we won't be able to mess with their minds as easily as we do in the human realm!"

Sharpclaw and Lenny stopped and looked at each other in shock and awe. It was Lenny that spoke hesitantly first.

"He has a point. If humans do come here, what will we do for fun? They'll know all about us!"

Sharpclaw was quiet as he thought it over. You could almost see the cogs turning in his head as he pictured the realm full of humans, stamping on everything and getting in the way.

"Every time something goes wrong, they'll blame the gremlins straight away and point their fingers at you and say 'Oh, it was old Sharpclaw that stole my socks or keys' and they'll come after you," mocked Scarlett.

"Okay, we have a truce, for now, Princess. We'll help you, but then we all go our separate ways. Deal?" said Sharpclaw.

"Deal!" said Scarlett and Pichael together.

CHAPTER THIRTY-FIVE
Unlikely friends

The little group carried on down the corridor until they found a stone staircase. The tower was very quiet as they tiptoed to the bottom, which seemed to take hours. Eventually, they arrived at a large wooden set of doors.

"This looks like an exit, but first you will need one of these each," said Sharpclaw, handing a tooth to everyone in the group.

"Tooth Bearer teeth, are they always warm to the touch?" said Pichael.

"Only if a Tooth Bearer is near," said Sharpclaw.

"How come you got them?" asked Lenny.

"I'm not stupid. I've never trusted Tiana, so I kept a few teeth for myself!" laughed Sharpclaw.

"These are Katelyn's teeth!" smiled Scarlett, holding one up to the light. "So that's what a baby tooth looks like then!"

"Well, they are going to serve us more than they do Tiana right now. What she doesn't know, don't hurt her!" said Sharpclaw, pushing open the large doors. He stopped suddenly, as he saw a figure before him, encased in an orb of green goo. "Someone's gift-wrapped a fairy, and left it on the door!" he said.

"Who is it?" asked Scarlett as she peered over Sharpclaw's shoulder. She quickly recognised her friend through the green gel and tried to grab the orb but it was too slippery and her hands kept sliding off the slimy surface. "It's Tilly, quick, help me get her inside where it's safe!" cried Scarlett, digging away at the goo.

"Nancy, I can see Nancy in her bag!" cried Pichael, as he tried to pull the goo off the little fairy.

"Help Tills? You have got to be kidding me. You'd have to pay me a coin first!" snapped Sharpclaw.

Both Pichael and Scarlett gave him a nasty look.

"First time for everything, eh Sharpclaw?" said Lenny as he nudged his friend.

"Okay, fine. I'll do it, but you owe me big time!" he said.

The four of them managed to drag Tilly out of the slime and back inside the safety of the tower. They closed the door and sank into a heap, tired out.

Tilly slowly returned to life, the colour returning to her face replacing the pallid complexion.

"Where am I?" asked Tilly, her voice faint and distant. They removed the last blobs of green goo from her body.

"Tilly, what are you doing here, is Katelyn with you?" asked Scarlett.

"Oh, my head hurts. Hello, have we met?" asked Tilly, staring blankly at the fairy.

"I'm Scarlett, you know me. I'm Katelyn's friend!"

"Katelyn, Katelyn…, that name rings a bell. Why do I know that name?" asked a confused Tilly.

"You know Katelyn, you're her tooth fairy!" said Scarlett.

Tilly looked completely confused.

Sharpclaw pushed Scarlett aside and said, "Do you remember who you are then?"

"My name is…, my name is?"

"Tilly, you have to remember!" cried Scarlett.

"…," Tilly looked blank.

"She's lost her mind. Best stick her outside again. Nothing we can do," said Sharpclaw, offhandedly.

"Can you be more helpful?!" snapped Scarlett.

"It's the Darkness of Disbelief, that's what it is. Give her a bit of time, maybe her memory will come back" said Pichael, trying to sound hopeful.

"I got stuck in the Darkness once. Didn't do me any harm" said Lenny, casually.

They all looked at him, the room was silent.

"Don't worry Lenny, you didn't lose anything that was never there in the first place!" said Sharpclaw.

"Let her have some air, I'm sure she'll be alright!" said Pichael to Scarlett, ignoring Sharpclaw's remark.

"I hope you're right, Pichael," a concerned Scarlett exclaimed, she looked sadly at Lenny.

Scarlett lifted Tilly's magical talisman. The stone within glowed with a warm white radiance. Without thinking, she placed Tilly's hands upon the stone. The clear gem glowed brighter and illuminated the room. Tilly glowed brighter and brighter, then the light dimmed and returned to normal.

Tilly opened her eyes as if for the first time.

"Scarlett, am I glad to see you!" she said.

Scarlett hugged the little fairy and cried with joy.

"Scarlett, what has happened to you?" cried Tilly as she pulled away from her friend, and realised that Scarlett had transformed into a fairy.

"A long story and one I don't really understand myself. I wanted to write the news, not make it!" said Scarlett, turning this way and that and showing off her wings.

"Katelyn, we have to save Katelyn. Toothsayer Tiana has her imprisoned in goo as well upstairs!" said Tilly, suddenly remembering her old friend.

"Save Cake Tin, hang on. I draw the line at saving the Tooth Bearer. If it ever got out that I'd helped her as well, then I'd be the laughing stock at the gremlin court!" cried Sharpclaw.

"Mister Sharpclaw!" said Pichael, glaring at him.

Scarlett clicked her fingers together as a plan formed in her mind.

"Look, I have an idea. Sharpclaw, Lenny, and Pichael can destroy the fairy ring, the Tooth Bearer teeth will protect them when outside. Tilly and I will go and rescue Katelyn and stop Tiana," commanded Scarlett, who quite enjoyed taking charge.

"Who upped and made you our leader for a day?" asked Sharpclaw.

"My dad did. King Pontin!" said Scarlett, with a smug grin on her face.

"Fair enough!" mumbled Sharpclaw.

They held the Tooth Bearer teeth for protection and opened the door again. The circle was almost complete and the shambling mound, known as Eartha, was just finishing planting the last few mushrooms. They sparkled in the purple light.

"How do we stop that?!" asked Lenny.

"Got any weed killer?" asked Sharpclaw.

"Remember the statue that Tiana held, I believe she controls the golem with it!" shouted Pichael.

"That window up there is where Katelyn is being held," said Tilly, as she pointed at the tower.

"It took us hours to climb down the stairs. Yet the window isn't that high up?" wondered Scarlett aloud.

"Perception isn't always a reality. I heard that grumpy Toothsayer say that once!" explained Pichael.

"We need to get up there fast, but how?" said Scarlett to Tilly, as she ran towards the door.

"Wait Scarlett, make sure you have a Tooth Bearer tooth for protection. I have an idea!" shouted Tilly.

"Am I going to like this idea of yours, Tilly?"

"We are going to do what fairies do best, Scarlett. We fly up!"

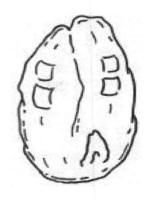

CHAPTER THIRTY-SIX
Thimbles and Needles

Katelyn tried to move but no matter how hard she pushed against the goo, it wouldn't budge.

"Wriggle all you want child, you won't get free!" smiled Tiana smugly. "Any minute now my golem will finish creating the largest fairy ring ever, and then the humans will start to arrive. So just relax, and prepare to meet and greet," said the Toothsayer.

Katelyn looked around the room, she had to do something, but what?

She looked at the desk where she saw the ugly statue and a bag of teeth. Tooth Bearer teeth.

Just then her hand brushed against something cool

to the touch in her pocket. It was Charlie's Seeing Stone, she had forgotten all about it, with everything else that had taken place. She started to hatch a plan in her mind. It might just work!

With difficulty, she managed to worm the crystal out of her pocket. She had one chance to do this.

Remembering what Tilly had told her, she thought of small things like ants and ladybirds.

WHOOSH!

Toothsayer Tiana turned around to see the green slimy orb sitting in her room. It was empty.

"IMPOSSIBLE!" she screamed. "You couldn't have vanished. You are an ordinary girl, not a mage. Where are you?!" snarled Tiana.

Katelyn climbed up into the space that she had previously occupied in the green orb. She was really tiny and was able to hide from the Toothsayer with ease. She ran across the floor towards the door.

"There you are. Don't think you can escape from me, little girl!" said Tiana and she pointed her finger at Katelyn. "Glaciate benumb!"

An icy blast flew over Katelyn's head and hit the wall in front of her, causing her to change direction and run towards the Toothsayer.

Just then Tilly and Scarlett appeared at the window. They climbed inside, eager to stop Tiana.

"What have you done with the Tooth Bearer?" shouted Tilly angrily, advancing on the Toothsayer.

"I see you have both escaped. I should give you more credit I suppose, however, I am afraid you are too late. The circle is complete. Prepare to greet your new Queen!" shouted Tiana. "Behold, the portal opens!"

"Thimbles and needles!" proclaimed Tilly.

CHAPTER THIRTY-SEVEN
The circle complete

Outside, the giant mud golem known as Eartha had completed its work and now stood guard. The mushrooms started to glow as each crystal within the fungus became charged with magic. A wind blew through the clearing and knocked the three gremlins off their claws.

"Come on we have to shred the mushrooms!" shouted Pichael, as a sheet of newspaper blew from the middle of the circle, where a magical portal was opening and caught him in the face.

"Watch out, human junk coming through!" shouted Sharpclaw, and he sprang through the air and landed on top of Eartha. The monolithic hulk spun around with the gremlin hanging on for dear life. It flailed its arms through the air, trying to grab the reptile but Sharpclaw dug his heels in.

"Not today, you walking compost heap!" said the gremlin as he traded blows with the golem. He had to keep out of the way of its huge arms, as one blow from Eartha would send him flying.

Lenny and Pichael pushed through the hurricane that was blowing, using their claws to gain a foothold in the ground, trying to reach the glowing fungus, and the portal that at any second would send humanity into another new realm.

Newspapers, bottles, and an old sandwich flew past the gremlins.

"Today please, I can't hold this pile of manure forever!" shouted Sharpclaw, his arms wrapped around the giant golem.

SNAP!

A tree branch flew through the portal and hit Sharpclaw and Eartha sending them barrelling into Lenny and Pichael. All of them ended up in a heap at the base of the tower.

Eartha was up first and towered over the three, scared gremlins. Its tree trunk-like fists raised in anger. Its face contorted into a vegetable patch of rage. Rotten, stinking vegetables appeared upon its torso.

"It's going to hit us with rotten cabbages!" shouted Pichael, trying to take cover before the vegetable barrage began.

"Take cover!" cried Lenny, and he dived behind Sharpclaw, just as the first old, stinky cabbage was cast at them.

Back in the tower, a triumphant Toothsayer Tiana gloated over the fairies before her.

"Scarlett, you could have had all this power and

ruled at my side. You could have been someone with power!" Tiana said with menace.

"I am someone. I AM ME!" screamed Scarlett.

"Scarlett, get behind me!" said Tilly.

"I don't want to rule. I like who I am and I want to go home to my daddy!" shouted Scarlett.

"So be it child, but others might not turn their heads so easily when asked. Remember, you are not the only absent crown!" hissed Tiana.

"What do you mean?" asked Scarlett.

The door opened and in walked Mister Beeching.

"Goodness, what a mess!" he said.

Tilly quickly used the distraction to jump towards Tiana. Although not a mage, she was still armed with her jar of sleep dust. She grabbed the jar, flipped the lid open, and tried to throw it at Tiana.

"Not so fast little tooth fairy. Do you take me for a fool!" snapped Tiana and she pointed a finger at Tilly and chanted, "Fulmination fireball!"

Tilly brought up her little pin sword for protection just in time as the bolt hit, sending sparks of lightning around the room as it bounced off the pin. The force of the bolt threw her backwards into the wall and she slumped to the ground.

"Ouch, that nearly burnt my wings off," she said.

Mister Beeching reached over and grabbed the tooth fairy firmly.

"Not so fast. Best you stay out of harm's reach!" he said.

Katelyn meanwhile ran towards the desk as fast as she could. The floor was cobbled and this slowed down her pace. Reaching the table she climbed up the leg, hoping to reach the top without being seen.

This was not like clambering up a climbing frame in the playground, however, and Katelyn kept slipping down the smooth wooden table leg. She felt like a tooth fairy trying to reach a well-hidden tooth.

"Next time I'm going to place my baby teeth somewhere easier to reach," she said to herself.

Scarlett noticed the tiny girl climbing towards the top and screamed, "Katelyn, smash the golem statue. Tiana controls the creature outside with it!"

Toothsayer Tiana spun around, and she saw Katelyn standing beside the crudely made statue, trying to kick it over. She was not having much luck as it was far too heavy for her little foot.

"Foolish Tooth Bearer, what do you think you are trying to do?" she shouted in a blind rage.

"STOP YOU!" responded Katelyn.

"Bravery will not get you anywhere today, child. This is one fairy story you will, regretfully, not finish. It is time to seal your fate, Tooth Bearer, fulmination fireball!" hissed Tiana.

"Katelyn..., WATCH OUT!" screamed Scarlett.

The molten ball of hot lava shot from Tiana's hand and streaked across the room, sending fiery red and orange flames in its wake as it roared towards the little girl.

Chairs were turned over and tables knocked aside as it flew towards its destination. The heat was intense.

Katelyn turned at the last minute, her eyes reflecting the approaching ball of flame.

"Oh no!" she uttered.

CHAPTER THIRTY-EIGHT
The final falling tooth...

"NO!" shouted Tilly, from where she was held.

The room lit up with a bright fire that blinded everyone and exploded in the area where the table stood. Papers and books flew into the air and the smell of scorched hair and parchment filled the room. Burning embers floated to the ground.

Katelyn jumped at the very last moment into the bag of teeth, as the fiery lightning bolt streaked across the room and hit the statue instead of Katelyn. It exploded into a hundred tiny pieces of burnt clay and mud.

Outside, for the first time, the golem known as Eartha roared a horrific scream. It stopped pelting the gremlins with vegetables and charged towards the portal, ploughing through the mushrooms and sending the fungus flying into the air. The moment the circle was broken the portal vanished, and the hurricane ceased.

Wailing, for the first time in control of its movements, Eartha charged into the forest and disappeared between the twisted trees.

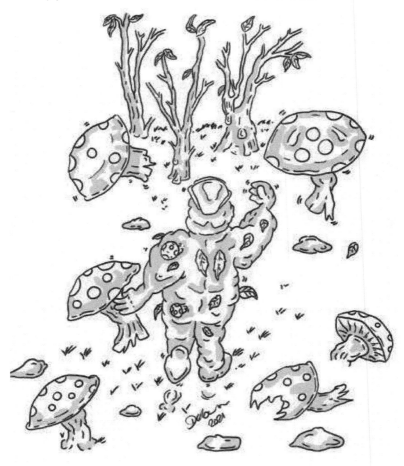

"NO!" shouted Tiana.

"WHAT,

HAVE,

YOU,

DONE!" she screamed at the little group of friends.

"We've stopped you in your tracks, Tiana. It's over!" shouted Tilly.

"IT IS NEVER OVER UNTIL I HAVE WON, FAIRY!"

Tiana fired another lightning bolt across the room, which exploded against the wall causing Mister Beeching and Tilly to duck quickly.

"It has only just begun. You haven't stopped me, Tilly Lightfeather. You have only delayed the inevitable. Trust me when I say that you have not seen the last of me. Our paths shall cross again!"

Mister Beeching released his hold on Tilly and smiled at the group, knowing what was to come.

"Train is ready to depart ma'am, shall we leave?"

Tilly spun around and stamped on his big toe, causing him to hobble around.

"My foot!"

He tried to knock Tilly over but she easily ducked and he hit the wall instead.

"Ouch, my thumb, you should respect your elders!" he shouted at Tilly, shaking his fist in the air.

"Respect should be earned, not just given," replied the fairy as she took off and sped towards Tiana. A streaking colour of green and red flew across the room aiming at the Toothsayer, determined to stop her.

Tiana looked up at the approaching tooth fairy and held up her hand causing Tilly to stop in mid-flight as if held in an unseen grip. She hovered in mid-flight, unable to move.

"Root cavity and dentures, I'm stuck like dental glue!" Tilly shouted.

Scarlett sprang across the room using her wings for momentum and tried to grab the Toothsayer, but Tiana waved her hand and uttered an incantation under her breath which pushed Scarlett over, sending her crashing into nearby red, velvet drapes that fell from their curtain poles on top of her.

Tiana pointed her finger directly at the red-headed girl. Her eyes blazed with fire and anger.

"Stop!" screamed a miniature Katelyn from the bag of teeth, causing Tiana to spin around and throw a fireball at the little Tooth Bearer. Luckily it struck the table sending books and the remaining parts of the golem statue flying into the air.

The thick smell of burnt wood filled Katelyn's nostrils and caused her eyes to stream with water so that she couldn't see.

She prayed that Tilly would be able to do something but what could she do, for she was held in the air like a model aeroplane on a string.

She could only shout from her little bag of teeth.

"Please Tiana, remember who you once were. Remember the kind tooth fairy that visited the children at Cottingley, don't let her disappear.

Please remember!"

Tiana once again turned her attention towards Scarlett who had pulled herself out of the curtains. The Toothsayer pointed her finger at the girl once again and prepared to fire.

"Fulmination fire..., NO. I once protected you and your family. I cannot destroy you, my princess. However, I will convince you and those that you love. In time you will all join me as you once did. Remember me, as I remembered you!" Tiana spoke softly, her voice almost as soft as the breeze that blew through the open window.

She lowered her arm and the glow from her hand faded. For a brief moment, it was as if Tiana had regained some of her former self and was once again the Toothsayer that had followed her king.

"Until we meet again Princess Scarlett. Please pass on my regards to your father!" smiled Tiana. She paused and took a breath, as if wanting to say something else but thought better of it.

Closing her eyes the Toothsayer grabbed her talisman that she wore around her neck, and chanted the words, "Evanesce vanish!"

A bright light emanated from the central crystal, held within the talisman. It became so bright that nobody could see anything, and the whole room smelt of cinnamon. Everyone covered their eyes.

As the light faded, so did Tiana's spells and the friends fell through the air as the tower, the train, Mister Beeching, and Toothsayer Tiana vanished completely.

Outside the three gremlins looked up as the train disappeared and was replaced by the two falling fairies and the bag of teeth containing Katelyn.

Down they fell. Scarlett tried to flap her wings but only managed to slow her descent.

"Ouch, use your wings and learn to fly!" shouted Sharpclaw, as Scarlett landed on top of him, sending him flying.

Tilly flew through the air and grabbed the falling bag of teeth that held Katelyn. "I guess this is how humans must feel when they meet us!" laughed Tilly, as she stared at the tiny Katelyn who sat within the canvas bag, holding onto the teeth for support.

"Did we win?" asked Katelyn from within.

"Yes we did!" replied Tilly.

The group landed within the broken clearing. Piles of smashed mushrooms lay about the floor, mixed with rubbish and items blown through the portal.

A newspaper here, a tree branch there.

"We did it, we stopped Toothsayer Tiana!" exclaimed Tilly happily.

"I can't believe it. We won!" said Scarlett.

"Excuse me! Can you let me out of the bag please?" asked Katelyn.

"Must you? I'd pay to keep her in there for another five minutes!" smiled a toothy Sharpclaw.

"Shame on you!" said Tilly, opening the bag so that Katelyn could climb out.

Katelyn scrambled over her teeth and jumped out. She saw Scarlett, properly as a fairy, for the first time.

"Scarlett, wow. I...," exclaimed Katelyn.

"I know, I didn't expect this either!" replied Scarlett.

Katelyn regained her composure at seeing her friend and said, "You're a fairy, but how..., when?"

"Trust me, Katelyn, I don't have a receipt for this one, I'll be on the shelf with a front-page story, but you won't buy it!" replied Scarlett. She took a look at the miniature Tooth Bearer before her and tried her best not to laugh.

"I just can't take you seriously at that size!" she

said, trying hard not to smirk. The pair couldn't contain themselves however and both laughed together, although Katelyn's voice sounded like a high-pitched squeak.

"Looking at you now though Katelyn, I think any story I have to tell will be very believable!"

Scarlett sighed deeply and took a breath, "I'm sorry I ran off earlier when we were in that city. It was wrong of me and...," Scarlett started to say as she regained her composure.

"Don't worry, I'm just glad we found you, we are a team," replied Katelyn. And gave her friend a hug as best she could considering her size.

"The Darkness of Disbelief, quickly everyone. We are not out of the woods yet!" shouted Tilly.

She held up the bag of teeth and shook it.

"Everyone, quickly crowd around the bag of teeth. They will protect us from the corruption!"

As they gathered around the cloth bag of Tooth Bearer teeth for protection, wondering how they would ever escape the forest, a bright light was seen on the horizon. It was very small.

It drew nearer and nearer, and soon the familiar shape and sound of the Spirit of Landon appeared, parting the dark, heavy clouds like velvet curtains.

"Ahoy there, need a lift?" shouted a voice.

"That's Charlie's voice, are we glad to see you!" shouted Katelyn as loudly as she could.

"Climb up the ladder!" a second voice was heard shouting and a small rope ladder descended towards the group like a lifeline.

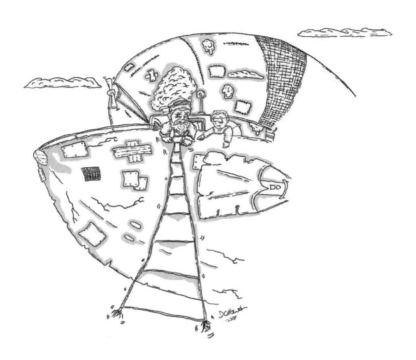

CHAPTER THIRTY-NINE

The journey home

There was much celebrating on the craft during the return flight as Stanley played the accordion, accompanied by Timoir on the fluteal, which is an ancient type of fairy flute. Pippa and Tilly baked more apple pies for their tea, and also just in case they ran into some more pirates again on the way home.

Katelyn was returned to the size of everyone else by Timoir and a handy Seeing Stone.

Charlie nearly fainted when he saw his friend Scarlett come aboard the ship. Her wings outstretched and edged with a tint of red that matched her hair.

Even Sharpclaw and Lenny enjoyed the return trip, asking to be dropped off at the Crescent City on the route home.

Pippa

by Katelyn London

Pichael spent the trip drawing on Nancy, filling her shell with images for her to see of their adventures. Scarlett meanwhile filled her time by taking photographs and trying out her new wings, whilst Katelyn took out her drawing pad and sketched her friends.

Very soon the lights of the city appeared on the distant horizon, it was good to reach a friendly port.

"Now that you are all safe and Tiana has gone, our deal is done. Until next time, Tills. You keep taking the teeth and we'll keep making mischief," said Sharpclaw with a toothy smile.

"Agreed, until we meet again. Take care and, I can't believe I'm saying this but..., thank you Sharpclaw and Lenny. We couldn't have done it without you" said Tilly, humbly.

"Think nothing of it, Tilly, it was fun," replied Lenny.

"Goodbye Princess Scarlett, I hope to see you again, soon," said Pichael as he picked up Nancy the egg and held her tightly.

"As do I, Pichael. Thank you so much for everything," said Scarlett, and she kissed him on the nose which made the little gremlin blush.

"Well Lens, no time like the present. Said Sharpclaw to Lenny, slapping him on the back.

"Bye, everyone. Watch your socks!" said Lenny.

"Hang on, one last thing. The Tooth Bearer teeth please!" jumped in Tilly, just as they were leaving.

"Rats, don't expect us to change overnight, will you Tills?" said Sharpclaw, as he grudgingly handed over the magical teeth that he had.

"Wouldn't have it any other way," said Tilly.

With a brief stop for supplies and repairs in the Crescent City, the Spirit of Landon took to the skies once more and headed for the capital City of Landon, passing fields and forests, towns and villages. The Darkness of Disbelief became a distant blot on the horizon, like an ink stain on a clean shirt. It would be dealt with over time.

"So what now?" said Katelyn to Scarlett, as they watched the world go by with Tilly and Charlie, "Will you stay and re-join the royal family here?"

"She'd better not because I'm not bowing all the time and pulling her chair out for her if I come to visit!" said Charlie.

"We would love to have you stay and learn from us. You could teach us so much as well," said Tilly.

"Of course I always knew the truth, saw it right away. It's the nose you see, same point at the end," said Pippa, carrying an apple pie from the galley below for everyone to share.

"I've decided to return home. I want to see so many things here, but I'm Scarlett Dorsey, and my dad runs the paper shop in town. That's who I am. My dad doesn't remember being the King, let alone being the Fairy King. It wouldn't be fair on him. I will come and visit though!" Scarlett told her friends.

She walked across the deck to where Toothsayer Timoir was sitting darning a sock for Stanley. She looked up and sighed, "With all the available magic, you'd think a darning spell would be created. What can I do for you, Scarlett?"

"Toothsayer Timoir..., I love that I have family here, but I cannot leave my dad, and he doesn't remember anything of his past. If he found out it might hurt him. I need you to cast a glamour spell and change me back into ordinary Scarlett, please?"

The Toothsayer stopped what she was doing and put down her mending.

"Nobody is ever ordinary, Scarlett, you are as unique as each new morning that dawns, and that will always make you interesting. I understand your wishes and will do as you desire. However, please allow this old Toothsayer the chance to look in on you from time to time. I feel I might even take out a subscription to your local paper."

"Of course!" said Scarlett and hugged Timoir, tears rolled down her cheeks. "Thank you!" she said.

Pippa stood watching with Tilly from a distance.

"I wonder what became of the Queen. She changed so much, yet she showed compassion at the end? Do you think that she can still be saved from herself?" Pippa quietly asked her niece.

The question remained unanswered, however, as a

shout was heard from the front of the ship.

"Land ho!" shouted Stanley from the wheelhouse as the flying ship docked at the capital city at last.

Everybody rushed to the side of the ship as crowds quickly gathered to welcome the group home.

There was much waving, cheering and jumping up and down from everyone, mostly from an over-excited Tilly, but above all else, there was a sense of relief. Once again Katelyn the Tooth Bearer had saved the realm with the help of her friends.

CHAPTER FORTY
Home

The next few days were a whirlwind for the three children. A celebration party was thrown at the palace with lots of dancing, and Pippa was able to serve up her world-famous pirate beating apple pies at long last. A national holiday was declared by King Stepney and Queen Clement, who were also able to get to know their long-lost niece at last.

The humans that had arrived through Tiana's fairy rings were all returned, however, rumours of a giant cat still persisted in the forested areas of the realm.

Stanley eventually returned the flying machine to his shed for repairs, very clearly enjoying the fame that now accompanied it.

"Where do you think Tiana went?" Katelyn asked Tilly. They were staying at the Crystal Palace for a few days and tonight, more so than ever before, the realm felt like it had a renewed hope. Like a weight being lifted off a person's shoulders.

"Her talisman would have carried her back to the human realm. If she returns here, then it will be to the spot where she departed. Like a bungee cord."

"I hope she gets caught soon. She scared me when she said she'd see us again. I'm really afraid!" said Katelyn, as she stared out over the balcony into the royal gardens.

"As am I Katelyn. We will always look out for each other though. We'll be fine, and if she returns, we will be ready," smiled Tilly.

"She did seem strangely familiar as if I'd met her before. Like I knew her," Katelyn mused.

"The Darkness affects people in many different ways. Tiana spent a long time in its shroud and it changed her. She...," Tilly paused and thought about her words carefully. "She wasn't always the person we met. Don't judge her actions harshly."

"Come on you two, stop chatting outside. Katelyn needs a good night's sleep for her return trip home," said Pippa cheerfully as she emerged onto the balcony behind her two friends.

"I am very tired, goodnight Tilly and Pippa. I'll see you in the morning."

When Katelyn had retired to her bedroom Pippa turned to Tilly. Her face held a heavy frown and she looked very stern. Tilly who was used to her aunt being constantly jolly only saw this face when a lecture was imminent.

"I know what you are going to say. I don't agree!" Tilly said sternly before her aunt could say anything.

"She doesn't need to know yet. The King requested that it be kept secret from the children, for now," replied Pippa.

"Both Katelyn and Scarlett should be told the truth. They have a right to know," answered Tilly angrily.

Pippa nodded sadly in agreement. "Yes, and they will but not yet. One step at a time. It's not often that I agree with Timoir but after speaking with her on this I do. Please, I beg you, keep it under your helmet until the time is right and Tiana returns to us. With luck as the good Tiana that we used to love, and not the darkness infected one we have to deal with now."

"When did you know that Scarlett was the daughter of King Pontin and Queen Tiana?" asked Tilly.

"I had an idea when we were in the palace looking at the paintings. She looked just like the old king, plus I could see a glowing aura around Scarlett. I just threaded the rest together until I spoke with Toothsayer Timoir," replied Pippa.

"An aura. You could see the magic?" asked Tilly, taking a step backwards in shock.

"Yes. So for now, please keep quiet. It could do more damage than good if the truth came out. Scarlett has been through so many changes, physically and mentally, it would hurt her. We need to allow her to get to know her new life first. Please?" asked Pippa taking her niece by the hand.

Tilly bit her lip and stared at her aunt. She kept silent but nodded her head.

"Thank you," said Pippa. The pair remained silent, both staring out over the lights of the capital city towards the darkness that covered the horizon.

A day later the children were home again in Haverhill, and the local police were tasked with sorting out the stories of people travelling to the land of magical fairies. Strange as the tales were, everyone was just happy to be back home.

Scarlett stood staring at her reflection in a mirror in her bedroom, whilst Charlie and Katelyn sat on bean bags. She tried to flap her non-existent wings.

"It's amazing that you can't see them. I feel like me again, but I do feel my wings as well. Perhaps I always felt them and just couldn't connect the dots. It's like a ghost pain I guess or if you wear glasses. You just get used to them," she said.

"I'd rather have wings than glasses. I could fly to school on time then!" said Charlie.

"As long as you're happy. Do you think you'll go back to the realm?" asked Katelyn.

"I hope so, as long as my two best friends go with me as well," said Scarlett smiling happily to herself.

She looked at herself in the mirror and the smile vanished to be replaced with a determined frown.

"That Tiana knew something. She wouldn't, or couldn't tell me what it was. Yet I felt something when I was with her..., a connection, sounds stupid doesn't it?" Scarlett asked.

"No, not at all, she was..., I mean is your Toothsayer," said Charlie looking up from his book.

"My mum is there, somewhere. Lost in the realm and I'm going to find her and bring her home. I don't care about the Darkness of Disbelief or magic or gremlins. I am going to find her and bring her home to dad and me!"

"Will you help me, please?" Scarlett turned and asked her two friends, who smiled warmly at her.

"Of course we will help you," said Charlie.

"Ready whenever you are!" smiled Katelyn.

Katelyn stood up from her bean bag chair and said, "Well Your Highness, we have a maths test in the morning and I have some drawing to do as well, so come on Charlie. We need to go home."

She hugged her friend goodbye and motioned for Charlie to get up and follow her.

"What do I say to your dad, I mean he's a king, I buy my weekly comic from him?!" asked Charlie. "Do I bow every time I pay him now?"

"You say goodbye Mister Dorsey, see you soon," said Scarlett, smiling happily in front of the mirror.

When her friends had left, Scarlett went over to her computer and plugged in her camera. Hundreds of photographs of a foreign, magical land were displayed. Fairies, gremlins, magical flying trains, and far-off cities were all there. She smiled to herself, her social media account was about to take off like never before.

"I will find you, Mummy!" she said to the mirror.

The next day Mister Walker, Katelyn's teacher, was collecting the test questions from the school desks. It had been a long day, but a good one, as the children had returned. Even if they couldn't recall where they had been.

"Hello, Jimmy!"

Mister Walker stopped and looked about. There was nobody but him in the classroom.

"Hello, anybody there?" he asked the room.

"Jimmy Walker, it has been a very long time. You've aged well, I have to say."

"Who's there, come out and stop playing games. School is closed for the day!" he said, spinning around in a panic.

"Jimmy, I can visit an old Tooth Bearer if I want to!"

Mister Walker span around and dropped the test sheets onto the ground, terrified.

"Who..., who are you?" he rasped, shaking with fear. A glow near his desk caught his attention.

"Why Jimmy, it's your old tooth fairy, Tooth Fairy Tiana. I have very much missed the little chats we used to have."

"I...," said Mister Walker.

"Now Jimmy, I need you to tell me where Scarlett Dorsey and her father live!"

THE

END

There are many illustrations of teeth throughout this story, but how many did you see?

Don't worry, you need not count all those teeth in the steam train tender!

If you have enjoyed reading 'The Tooth Bearer and the Masked Crown' then why not read the first book in the series, 'The Tooth Bearer'.

I would love it if you left a review of the books as this helps to raise awareness of the series.

Please also join my Illustrator and Author page where you will find updates and drawings of all the characters from the series and news of future books.

Thank you for reading and we will see you soon in the next chapter of 'The Tooth Bearer' series.

ABOUT THE AUTHOR

David Howden was born in Cambridge and would spend his early years touring the many music shops for jazz records. From an early age, he loved drawing cartoons for himself and his friends.

The Tooth Bearer was his first book which gave him the chance to combine his love of drawing and storytelling in one.
He lives in Suffolk with his wife Debbie and his daughter Katelyn, who went on all these adventures held within these pages.

If you have enjoyed reading this book then please offer support by leaving a review and following David Howden Illustrator and Author on Instagram and Facebook for future updates.
Why not visit the beginning of Katelyn's adventures in The Tooth Bearer, available in either illustrated or text-only versions.

The adventure continues for Katelyn and Tilly in the next thrilling chapter of the Tooth Bearer series, coming soon…